The Death of the Little Match Girl

BY ZORAN FERIĆ

TRANSLATED BY TOMISLAV KUZMANOVIĆ

AB Autumn Hill Books
Iowa City, Iowa

With the compliments of
Autumn Hill Books
www.autumnhillbooks.org

ÆB

http://www.autumnhillbooks.org

Autumn Hill Books, Iowa City, Iowa 52244

© 2007 by Autumn Hill Books
All Right Reserved. Published 2007

Printed in the United States of America

Originally Published as *Smrt Djevojčice sa žigicama*
© 2002 Zoran Ferić

Publication of this work was supported by the
Ministry of Culture of the Republic of Croatia.

Autumn Hill Books ISBN - 13:978-0-9754444-5-0
Autumn Hill Books ISBN - 10:0-9754444-5-x
Library of Congress Control Number: 2007932337

Contents

Angel Offsides

I made an unforeseen visit to the island to mourn an unexpected death and attend a child's funeral. I even bought a wreath — a futile effort to frame the emptiness with flowers — and with it like a cross on my shoulder, I climbed the stone path to the cemetery atop the hill. My friend's daughter had died. Her coffin was small and white, no bigger than a kitchen water heater box, and on that little white coffin was a wreath of white roses with a white sash and gold letters: TO MIRNA FROM MUMMY AND DADDY. The white lace, in which the six-year-old had been wrapped as if at baptism, was sticking out of the coffin. God loves irony. All this white was not accidental. Her father was a Hajduk fan.

In the homeland all our mortuary chapels look the same. Naked to the waist, their Amazonian breasts protruding, four varnished oak Graces hold the coffin, while the deceased rests on their arms. As if he's just scored a goal and is being carried to centerfield, where instead of Agnus Dei everyone will cheer: *Let's go, white!*

The father's face was contorted in horrible pain, like in that distant '74 when the club from Stara Plinara sustained a decisive upper left corner goal in the Champion's Cup. The gods of the soccer field, which was next to the old gas plant, Jerković, Šurjak, Mužinić and Žungul, front liners all, fell to their knees as if synchronized and buried their faces in their hands, hiding them there for a long time. Somebody yelled from the stands, "Your kid dying is better than whites losing!"

The kid was now an angel among angels. Even when she'd been alive, the color of her eyes had reminded you of that bright blue that's used to frame notices of children's deaths. It means heaven to children.

"If they die before their first period," our teacher used to say, "girls go directly to heaven, poor little things. They skip Purgatory." She'd been told this, supposedly, by her village priest.

The coffin, meanwhile, had been pushed in front of the chapel, where a microphone stood. It was then, I think, that something strange happened. A grizzled gentleman, whom I'd had the honor of seeing on the ferry deck, en route to the island, brought out a doormat and placed it discretely on the cart next to the coffin.

"That's Leichenbegleiter," a man standing next to me whispered in my ear.

"Excuse me?"

"Leichenbegleiter," the fellow repeated, "Corpse chaperon. If you haven't heard of him yet, you will."

I nodded, pretending to understand, and looked toward the platform where the coffin lay. From the side a bulky friar came waddling up. He turned toward the coffin, crossed himself, leaned over the microphone and began his eulogy.

But nothing could be heard. Silence!

The friar was opening his mouth like a goose fish in a crate, but there was no sound. The priest's assistant came running in a panic and began to fumble around the microphone. He tapped the membrane lightly and uttered one, one, one as if there were no twos or threes in the world. And the friar clasped his hands together and prayed for deliverance from such mechanical phenomena.

The devilish device finally showed mercy, setting the priest's words free. And his voice thundered above our heads, the vineyards, and the parks.

"Brothers and sisters," it boomed, "at moments such as this we ask ourselves: If God exists, why does he let little children die?"

An odd line for a priest to take. How would he exculpate himself on high when the time came?

But the canny cleric managed it in the following sentence, his heavenly employers in mind. "Even death, my brothers and sisters… is from God. Our sister, our little girl, our angel"—just then, as though nobody would notice, he fished a little crib sheet out of his gown, glanced at it with his discrete Franciscan eyes, and went on—"our *Mirna* rests now among the angels as one of them. When she was alive, she played on the streets and squares of our town, her happy voice echoed through her home…."

While the hallowed speaker talked about her short life, baptism, hop scotch, and various foolish things that children do, the audience wept in chorus. And there was no one who did not shed a tear for the repose of our sister's soul, for Mirna, dead from leukemia at the age of six. May she rest in peace.

2 TOMO'S TEARS; OR, WE'RE ALL WATER

After the priest's cathartic "Amen" at the end of the sermon, a certain commotion within the masses at the funeral could be felt, a moment of relaxation, like what happens at political rallies when the next speaker hasn't yet taken the stage. One name streamed through the audience in a whisper: Tomo, Tomo,

Tomooooo... But Tomo could not be found anywhere.

"He's taking a whiz," some soul mate of Tomo's explained. "He'll be here soon. Here he comes!"

And here was Tomo, making his way through the crowd and wiping the sweat from his forehead. Tomo the man, who used to be the most handsome of us all, irresistible to women. They said he had "fucked half Europe" and would go far. But he became a fisherman, took up Christ's work, feeding sardines to the people. He married his first cousin and had a mongoloid daughter. He was our next speaker.

Tomo positioned himself in front of the microphone, his stature broken, dark Ray Bans on his face to hide the tears, a black tie on a sweaty shirt. Noble water from the eyes. Smelly water from the armpits. The sea in the distance.

"Human life is like a river," he began, his voice quivering with fright because the whole town was listening. The flies were buzzing, the crickets singing from the cemetery park, and he, Tomo, a common fisherman, was speaking before his whole Renaissance town, which had once, a long time ago, even given birth to two renowned poets.

"From its source to its mouth," he went on, "it flies by in the blink of an eye! When we bury a man, we bury dust in dust. When we bury a sailor, we bury him in the sea: water in water. When we bury a soccer player: we bury him under the green!"

The audience was silent and uneasy. Something was wrong.

"Tomo! Left pocket. Left pocket!" somebody volunteered.

In a panic Tomo felt for the left pocket of his black tuxedo, which he had borrowed from his waiter brother-in-law, and took out another piece of paper. He looked at it, terror-stricken, as if he could not believe his eyes.

The man next to me said, "That was for the deceased Mrkela, a fisherman and a local goalie. His funeral's tomorrow. Both speeches were written by Pipo, the teacher."

Tomo awkwardly muttered several words of excuse and directed his attention to the other paper. And the town, the home of two poets, was quiet. Only the blowflies buzzed, flying down on the faces of the people and drinking their sweat.

Then he righted himself, wiped his eyes under the dark glasses, and began his recitation:

> *Your face was never met by darkness*
> *Nor will death disturb its memory,*
> *You have always been and will always be*
> *In our hearts and in our souls.*

After the word souls, the whole chapel choir began singing their favorite song: *Moj galebe.* Tomo, standing still before his town, took off his glasses and cried openly.

The scene was moving because we all knew he was crying for himself. People at the local taverns had long been saying he and his wife were lighting candles for St. Anthony that he should take that little girl of theirs, the Down Syndrome kid, as soon as possible. They'd put her dead uncle's earring, a present from before her birth, on her ear. The poor little thing can't even eat by herself, though her appetite is so big she could eat a cow. And then she soils herself in bed. They have to put diapers on her even though she's already seven. Severe retardation. And here somebody else's daughter had died. The injustice!

In those bright days at the end of May, when the tourist season was just beginning, we exhibited Muki's dick to the German women for a pack of Opatijas. The moron's lower echelon was distinguished by one deformity: his testicles did not come down from his abdomen, and his penis itself was not longer than three or four centimeters. Ulriche from Mainz, with whom I later fell in love, though others fucked her, pronounced an epochal sentence: *"Das ist der kleineste Schwantz im Europe!"*

After Tomo, Mukela, whom we called Muki for short—a local fool and boat farer, who'd been unsuccessfully going to Rijeka for the past ten years to take the test that would have allowed him to operate the boat he'd been operating for the past fifteen without the test—climbed onto the platform. Even Muki, who yodeled in the local port and so impressed the German tourists, even he had a deep inner urge to say goodbye to little Mirna. His obese dough-like body in shorts and rubber Jugoplastika flip-flops facing the microphone made everybody in the audience laugh. His face with its several double chins, and his handlebar moustaches were reminiscent of drawings of Balzac. He even began in a Balzacian manner, by unrolling a piece of paper as if it were a parchment scroll and reading: "This unfortunate little girl reminded one of a plant with its leaves turned yellow, one just planted in barren soil. Had she been lucky and turned twenty, she would have been magical. Fortune is the poetry of women, as dresses are their ornaments…"

Then Mirna's mother, moved by the dull-witted kindness, began crying and almost collapsed to the ground, while two old hags, like caryatides, supported her left and right.

"His dick may be small, but he's got balls!" commented somebody, respect in his voice.

Muki's yodeler speech prompted admiring silence. Many hands patted his sweaty shoulders when he came down to the crowd like a hero, a Cicero among the morons and a message to the people: kindness requires no brains.

4 RENATA

The tragic figure of the crying mother with the old hags as supporting pillars suddenly vanished from our sight. People looked around in surprise. Obviously they were not used to child funerals from which the mother unexpectedly disappeared.

"Poor woman must have gotten sick," said the old lady next to me.

"You're a doctor, aren't you?" said the Leichenbegleiter expert and pulled me by the sleeve. "We should go check what's happened to her."

We made our way around the grieving crowd and found ourselves behind a small stone chapel. A strange sight: Mirna's mother squatting and those women shielding her with their bodies. Her black skirt was pulled up and we could see her white underwear distinctly. One woman held her hand, probably for balance, while the other passed her the tissues.

"You never know how your bowels will react," my guide said. He made it sound like an apology.

The old women tried their best to hide her, but my eyes met hers. There was no shame in them. She looked at me with those watery blue eyes I knew so well. They'd looked at me like that more than fifteen years before in the park behind Villa Marijan when we were still in love. That summer she'd just finished middle school and I my sophomore year. I'd experienced magical, childish love with Renata, and my first French kiss on the terrace of the asthma clinic.

Disaster came with the first September rains, when I'd returned to Zagreb. My mother died. Renata was the only bright light in that tremendously long year, and her letters gave me a reason to go on. The thought of the summer, the strange shape of the island on the map, the smell of tanning oil, all that would come to me suddenly like a chest spasm during those gray, utterly identical days. And then summer came and I saw my love again.

She was now a head taller than me. She had stretched immensely during that year, and I somehow had stayed the same. The tricky charms of puberty. It surprised us both. We said hello, chatted a little, but my love was conserved and unrealized as if for a dead person.

5 LEICHENBEGLEITER

"This man," I asked my neighbor and guide through the local fauna, "this Leichenbegleiter, did he bring back Mirna's body from the hospital in Rijeka?"

"Oh, no," said the fellow. "He's a doctor. They call him Leichenbegleiter for fun. He was the kid's doctor. People say many of his patients have died. That's why they call him that."

"But who came with the coffin then?"

"The parents. They came with her, poor little thing. They were told the coffin couldn't go on the ferry unaccompanied, without a live escort."

"So what's he doing here?"

"He came to say goodbye to Mirna because he was once in love with her mother. From back when she was in college in Rijeka."

"And the doormat?"

"His name is Jungwirth. He's from a well-known family of doctors. He had the highest death rate in Rijeka hospital. Now everybody calls him Leichenbegleiter because he breaks bad diagnoses to patients. All his colleagues from the hospital in Rijeka and even from Susak send him their terminally ill patients so he can break the news."

"That's gruesome."

"My niece works there as a nurse so she knows all about Jungwirth. This conveying of diagnoses to patients became so routine to him with the years that he started having fun with it. He bought a doormat from some Gypsies, a regular woven doormat, my niece says, and put it inside his office door. When he tells someone he's got cancer or leukemia, he watches carefully to see if the person, who's been confused by the news, wipes his shoes when leaving the office. People say he keeps a very precise record of this: first name, last name, type and stage of illness, possible prognosis, and on the bottom of every file: 'wiped' or 'didn't wipe.' My niece says they usually wipe, particularly those with metastases. It's some kind of cleansing for them."

"If you listen to him, you're a bigger nut than he is," said the old lady next to my neighbor. "He starts in with the lies the moment he opens his mouth."

"Don't listen to the old hag," whispered the neighbor. "She's jealous because she doesn't know this stuff. There's more. He was in love with Renata, Mirna's mother, and he was greatly struck when he saw her in his office. He had to give her the terrible diagnosis about the child: Alzheimer's leukemia. There was nothing to be done. She had six months at most. And then he let her, too, all in tears, wipe her shoes. She wiped for quite a while, rubbed her shoes against the jute surface. That hurt: to watch the woman he once loved say goodbye. And it was all the doormat's fault. So now he wants to bury it together with the kid, as if it was some mean part of himself."

6 FATHER

My friend, the dead girl's father, had wished she was a boy. The two of them would have looked forward to the spring when the soccer playoffs began. He would have taken her to Poljud Arena to see an inspired Zoran Vujović playing in the opponents' penalty area. What would happen to her now in heaven's open fields, where all sorts of wishes come true? Would she grow a tiny wee wee?

The dead girl's father was German by origin, the son of a foreign woman who married an islander. I once observed how methodically and carefully he washed his toes, and it made me think about the high quality of German goods. Even later he was the same. Sound in all aspects: in high school he never had to take a make-up exam; he graduated from college right on time; he was sympathetic to friends and kind to acquaintances; he didn't fool around with the German girls; and, most important, he didn't masturbate.

He played attacking midfielder, although some thought he was a better center midfielder. He always kept his cool, playing smart, not with passion like the rest of us southerners. He swore silently and seldom waved his hands. He never spat on the asphalt field or smeared spit with his sneaker. To many this was a sign he was a good man. He controlled the ball with confidence, ran in big strides and all his teammates could see his intentions from afar. With him there were no surprises, hysterical body jerks, or illogical moves that confused his teammates as much as the opponents. As a player he was calm, composed, rational.

He got his nickname thanks to a T-shirt he wore in the '78 and '79 seasons, which had a smiling globe with a Hajduk fan cap with a sign on it: "The whole world loves Split!"

That T-shirt, local legend says, brought him good luck in all the island tournaments, including the one in the summer of '78 when our boys beat the Mali Lošinj team seven to one in the Kvarner League Championship. When his wife got pregnant with little Mirna, he was sure he'd be leaving the T-shirt to a son, as American fathers leave their baseball bats to their boys. When his daughter was finally born and the news that she was irrevocably and definitively a she reached the Alibaba Inn, somebody broke the impenetrable silence with a life-saving sentence: "Globus! What're you so uptight about? Hell, even girls play soccer these days."

7 FATE

"It's all fate," said the strip club owner's father, deeply moved, looking at Mirna's little coffin.

"I'm not sure I believe in fate," I replied.

"But have you heard of the woman who was dying from cancer in the middle of Auschwitz? Well, that woman is the best evidence you can get. Lying in a barrack in C Camp, right next to the gas chambers, she slowly faded away. I read it in Christian Bernadac's *Ninth Circle*. All of it's based on true testimonials. Other prisoners cooked porridge for her from the undigested kernels of corn from ss toilets."

"The guards never found her?"

"No. She died a natural death. Screwed over Hitler and Goebbels and all of them."

"Pssssssssssssssssttt," the old lady warned, "don't you swear at a child's funeral. Her classmates are about to sing her favorite song."

And there they were, children lined up next to one another by height on the platform before the chapel; boys first, then girls. They wore white shirts and navy trousers or skirts.

"Who could have said that one day all of them would...," began the owner of the strip club. "Who knows what we're fated for?"

"How's your wife?" I asked, changing the uncomfortable subject.

"She died three years ago. Intestinal strangulation," he answered as the Vladimir Nazor grade school chorus began a sad coastal song about the parting of a sailor and his gal. Mirna was the sailor. They were all the gal, seeing off their mariner to an uncertain destination.

"There are other, similar cases," he whispered. "When I was in the army, some captain, Radovanović was the name, tried to kill himself with a gun. He was on duty. The bullet went in through his temple and came out through his eye. He lived, his wife came back to him. He's got grandchildren now. He entertains them with his glass eye ball."

Meanwhile, Mirna's mother had finished her business and returned to her pedestal: tall, blonde, dignified. I marveled at not having been able to love a woman so much taller than me.

8 ANGELS

The children now sang La Cucaracha. Why? Mirna's mother's favorite song. The nostalgic memory of those long gone island days came back to me. Out of nowhere the cheerful rhythms brought a tiny breath of Mexican mountains and the spirit of the postseason on the Hotel Imperial terrace, where we'd picked out the remaining young German girls from among the rough skinned seniors. La Cucaracha made us all cry, and we sniveled in chorus while the children sang as one voice, and the music teacher, a certain Turkulin, his back to the grieving multitude, just waved his hands back and forth because the kids already knew it all by heart anyhow.

And then a strange commotion all of a sudden.

A girl from the first row knelt down on the stone ground and caressed it with her palms. Her classmates whispered to each other, and the tune of the song became dissonant. Now two more girls were squatting, running their fingers over the ground, as if there was Braille inscribed in the rocks. A boy from the last row circled the whole chorus with careful steps and joined the children caressing the ground. Some were still trying to sing, but most just managed to keep themselves from laughing. The children closed their mouths, giggling, and the song died out completely, giving way to the coughs and sniffles of the audience. A woman climbed up from the audience to the platform and questioned the children. A whisper spread among the people: "Lost her contact lens!"

Everybody seemed to understand and feel relieved. True, it was awkward but contacts were expensive. You had to go all the way to Rijeka for them. I learned that she was the mother of the little girl who'd lost her lens, and watched as she helped them search. The remaining children took this as a sign and got down as well. Little white shirts and navy trousers milled about Mirna's coffin, while Renata stared into space. She didn't see the little problems of the little children. Her eyes, may she be forgiven, wandered off into eternity, as if she stood behind frosted glass.

The atmosphere in the audience changed. Some people smiled, others tried to control their outbursts of laughter. Unsuccessfully, of course, as if they were fighting against metastases. It was all like a balloon filling with air, about to burst, when a child called out, "Here it is!"

She carried something we could not see on her finger, but we knew what it was, and she gave it to the mother of the reckless loser, who spread out a white hanky, wrapped up the lens, and, unaccustomed to her high heels, very gingerly descended into the smiling audience. The little children laughed too, standing in small undifferentiated globs around the coffin.

"Little angels!" observed the old lady next to me. "They don't know it's a sin."

And it seemed that a part of us all had fallen and hidden itself among the stones in the red dirt choked with cemetery weeds. The worst kind of weeds of all, for we know what feeds them.

9 THE SAWYER

The official program had ended, and there appeared to be no more speakers. The cemetery chapel was just about to sound the funeral march, for it was time, when some trembling unshaved young man climbed onto the platform before the chapel. Nobody seemed to recognize him.

"That's Ranko, from the Pipići family. He's not all there," said my neighbor, who was obviously well acquainted with all the island secrets. Now I remembered him too. Ranko, Foreign Legion admirer, who'd gone into the world in search of war. He'd worn army shirts, NATO hats and American Marine boots in the middle of summer. Center field defender.

By then he had spat and cleared his throat for the first word.

"People and ladies," he began ceremoniously, "little Mirna was chain-sawed in half. The poor little thing was playing with her dolls when they came and began cutting her."

Shock and horror spread through the crowd.

I could not get the picture of a little girl cut in half by a chain saw out of my head. A girl cut in half by a chain saw would be, first of all, short. If some time had passed since the cutting, her skin would be like plastic. A piece of the spinal cord extends from the spine, like that of a roasted lamb.

Ranko the rogue went on:

"The child was playing in the garden, in front of the cellar, when *they* came. One carried a chain saw, the other gas. They caught the kid and the one with the chain saw said, 'Two hundred Deutsch Marks or I cut!' I said, 'People, for God's sake, you wouldn't touch a Christian child. And I don't have any Marks.'"

"Get him down!" screamed somebody from the audience.

"Didn't she die because her blood went rotten?" an old lady called in my ear, confused.

But Ranko kept his poise and went on babbling. "They placed the kid on the table in the courtyard. The two of them held her, and the third one was about to start the chain saw. He

pulled the crank, but the saw wouldn't start. 'That's God help-
ing the poor thing,' I said to myself and prayed. Then the one
with the saw yelled: 'Stojan, get the gas!'"

The director of the psychiatric asylum and another doctor
climbed onto the platform. They took sawyer under his arms
and dragged him down.

"Ranko, calm down," said the doctor. "You only dreamt all
that, Ranko, it's not real."

"It's real. Real, I tell you." Ranko replied. "But these here
don't know it's real."

"For God's sake, who let him out?" yelled the director. More
people stepped in and led the man away, nearly carrying him.

Then silence. The wind in the pines. The crickets singing.

IO A PUZZLE

The graceful procession set out at last. The priest was first,
the little children with wreaths followed him, then the brass
band, the cart with the coffin, and, at the end, the grieving
crowd. Everything was in order: the men went first, the women
second, the mixed crowd followed. Maskarin walked next to
me. We'd been friends once. He'd married, divorced, married
again.

"You feed them and dress them," he said, his eyes on the coffin. "First diapers, then little kids' porridge, then picture books,
school books. Do you know how much a school bag is? With
cat's eyes. And a pencil case? A lot of money, Fero, big bucks.
And then she up and dies on you."

"I understand," I said. I really did. He had three kids. All
living. It wasn't easy for him.

The doormat came into view again. As the cart shook, the rascal fell off. A confusing moment for the cemetery personnel because they didn't know whether they should stop or not. A delicate little woman, dressed casually, in jeans and a black T-shirt, saved the situation by running to the cart and putting the doormat back in its place. Then she discretely re-joined the procession.

"Isn't that yours?" Maskarin asked, indicating the small woman.

"My what?" I asked though I knew what he was talking about.

"Did you ever even screw her?"

She was a widow. That was all I knew about her back then. Taught Croatian at the local high school.

"I thought she'd left the island," said Maskarin. "You remember when Pipo and me used to fuck around with her head? She'd go nuts."

I remembered. Who could forget, I said to myself. She used to read Petrarch to us passionately, while Pipo and Maskarin jerked off into their hankies under the desk. She loved me because I wrote good compositions. Even invited me home for tea a couple of times and told me I would become a great poet. We never went further than a kiss, and she never once mentioned her late husband.

"What happened to her husband?" I asked.

"Died in a train accident. They talked about burying them all in a common grave in Zagreb, but he somehow wound up here. He wasn't really in one piece."

"How's that?"

"They wanted to bury them in a common grave because they couldn't put them together. A leg here, an arm there, and a nose nowhere. They had to go look for the nose all around the crash scene, but it had flown all the way to the Branimir Market. Or else: they finally managed to put together all the parts, two arms, two legs, and then they ended up having two different shoes on the body. But the pants were the same. Either the guy was crazy and put on whatever came into his hands first, or two guys bought the same pants on sale. So what could they do? They sliced some skin off his shin and sent it to the lab for analysis. 'Why don't we take his shoes off?' suggested one of the doctors for the dead at Šalata Hospital. So they took off his shoes. What a sight—one leg shorter, but still it might have been his. They took off his socks. No toes on his left foot, two missing ones on his right. Bottom line: two toes. Fuck it, a diabetic! Every morning he gives himself a shot of insulin and once in a while they cut off a toe. We did some calculating: if after cutting each toe off the period before the next amputation was lessened by a year, and his first toe was cut off when he was fifteen, the second one when he was twenty, how old was he when he died?"

"She wasn't old," I said. That was all I could say in her defense. Perhaps in mine too.

"At the identification she didn't recognize him by his face, which was completely scorched. But she knew by those crippled feet of his. That's why he had to wear different shoes. Imagine, every time he had to get two pairs. Expensive. She was relieved when he died."

"I understand," I said. And I really did. Not only because of the expense.

When she was leaving the island, we met for the last time at Škver next to Vela Stina. It was the beginning of September and the figs getting ripe.

"That's the way it has to be," she said and kissed me on the forehead. She had to stand on her toes to reach me with her lips. I thought how my mother, had she been alive, would have also had to stand on her toes to kiss me. After that she began to cry. I took the hanky from my pocket and gave it to her. Reckless.

"It's wet," she said. "Have you been crying?"

But as she raised it to her face to wipe her tears, she stopped for a moment and smelled it. I watched her nose crinkle and relax, as if before a sneeze, trying to work out the origin of the scent hidden in that piece of fabric.

"You pig!" she finally uttered. "It smells of semen!" And the hanky, which she'd thrown away, slowly fluttered to the ground.

As she was leaving, I wanted to tell her, openly and honestly, that that's how men cry, but I didn't. And as her back gradually turned into a black dot under the city walls, I stood at that same place aware that I would remember that picture as long as I lived.

11 PHOTOGRAPHS

Meanwhile, the procession reached the open grave, dispersed and turned into an irregular circle whose center was once again the chubby Franciscan. The gravediggers, including the drunken Antoni, who often pissed himself, fumbled with the ropes, as if untying a boat. While they were undoing their own metaphysical knots, the audience sniffled and sighed. The most difficult moment had come: the coffin slowly disappeared into the red dirt. They'd dug the grave for an adult, and Mirna's little coffin looked strange in it. As if pirates were burying a chest.

In the meantime, the Franciscan began his speech. For the second time. "The people who had walked in the darkness saw a great light. A reading from the Epistle of St. Paul to the Corinthians..."

His voice seemed to make the tips of the cemetery cypresses sway, and all of us, believers and skeptics alike, crossed ourselves in obedience.

Mirna's mother had hired a photographer for the funeral. And he, at this solemn moment, cruised around our grieving personas clicking his little Japanese box. If I'm not mistaken, he clicked more around the better known town's people: the pharmacist, the guardian of the Franciscan monastery, the director of the psychiatric asylum, and the owner of the strip club. He had already snapped them a couple of times, as far as I'd seen. Then I noticed a thin Franciscan avoiding the lens, hiding behind some broad bereft shoulders. Suddenly I recognized that face: it was Friar Marijan, Ambrozije Testen's disciple from St. Euphemia's Monastery, a painter. He couldn't stand photographs. But I was certain that he was in a way recording, memorizing everything—the positions of the people, the colors (the contrast between the red dirt and the ivory coffin), the clothes, the constellations of clouds. And when he'd gone back to his cell, he would paint them unskillfully like a child and everything would resemble a painting made by some eight-year old. It seemed all of us were taking pictures, recording, memorizing, collecting impressions like children collect soccer players' photos. All that shooting was sickening. It wouldn't have surprised me to see our funeral photographs exhibited in the window of the only island photo shop—perhaps even under the heading, "The Team of '92", which was the year the island team had seen one of its historic moments, in the play-offs when they'd beaten Cres and Mali Lošinj two to one and three to nothing—all of us glued onto a blank double sheet of drawing paper, exposed to view like in some photo album, our serious faces looking into the distance.

The Franciscan, meanwhile, brought the sermon to its end by saying, "And now, let us pray for the first among us to depart after our sister!"

We all lowered our heads and murmured the prayer thinking, "It's not my turn, I hope." He closed his prayer book and sprinkled the holy water. One of the gravediggers took the doormat off the cart and placed it in front of the hole.

"See," said the old lady who appeared next to me again, "the child's daddy thought of everything. He brought that so we wouldn't get dirt on our shoes."

The grieving approached the grave, stepped on the doormat and threw in clods of red dirt, which thudded against the coffin. I watched them. When they'd dropped their clods, they would carefully wipe their shoes, as if ridding themselves of the contagious red dust, clean it from their raw persons and swim into a new life. All in vain! Like the earring on the girl with Down Syndrome.

The Death of the Little Match Girl

I THE GAME

Lately Jesus had been coming to Earth only in profanities. Soccer made the point. Tomo, Maskarin, Mungos and I were playing the first match of the 1st County League's Fall Championship against the Vultures from Cres, when Tomo suddenly yelled, "You fucking Jesus dick!"

Only half an hour before, at the Church of St. Euphemia, he'd melted a Franciscan wafer in his pious mouth, after Friar Marijan, now at goalie, had carefully placed it on his tongue. It was Sunday, 11 A.M., the sun was already scorching, and a light breeze was the only thing that cooled our sweaty faces. At the mention of Jesus' genitals, the friar, who had replaced his brown habit with a black goalkeeper's jersey, just crossed himself and rolled his eyes. He knew Tomo didn't think that seriously, and Jesus in a soccer game and Jesus in church were two completely different divine persons. As if a third of our Lord had suddenly turned schizophrenic. Besides, Tomo had two good reasons for swearing: first, it wasn't his daughter who'd died, and second, they'd just scored another goal in our lower left corner. That was three to one for the Vultures from Cres, whose team was in part sponsored by the Griffon Vulture Preservation Association. All this was on our home field, which for the occasion had been cleared of the few remaining cars—it served as a parking lot during the tourist season. The field usually passed through two unequal seasons: the tourist, boring and long, and the soccer, important but short. This match marked the beginning of the short season.

Unfortunately, we were two down because we were incomplete: Globus, whose daughter had been buried three days before, was missing. And he was our best striker. Nobody of course expected him to show up at the field that day because his house was still full of people expressing their condolences. They'd come, have a shot of brandy, sit silently on the patio and just once in a while say something like "It's God's will" or "Be strong." Renata and his mother only cleared away the glasses for Lozovača, washed them automatically like two machines with arms and legs, and then lined them upside down on the edge of the table covered with a colorful, fruity plastic tablecloth. On the first day Globus had said when the mourners came he'd just stare into the tablecloth, into the colors, because he couldn't look at the black of those ties and scarves anymore. Renata, on the other hand, gazed somewhere into the distance, far away from this island and its shore, somewhere beyond the sea where she used to go shopping for summer jeans and sandals as a little girl. Their eyes had not met since the kid had been buried.

The referee whistled the end of the first half, and we went dispirited to our bench. Mungos, a former classmate, now captain at the island police station, said, "Did I ever tell you my father played against the Russians in Hungary during the war?"

We all knew he'd said it just to break the depressing silence in which we dragged our tired bodies toward the bench, where a disappointed coach awaited us. But we hadn't heard the story. And he went on and on about how his father had been mobilized by the Partisans while he was in high school in Mitrovica and how they'd sent him together with some other units to Hungary to prepare for a breakthrough on the Srijem Front with the Russians. He was completely immersed in the story, as if we weren't two goals down. He said one Sunday morning they'd played in some demolished Hungarian village against the Russians with a ball made of old army coats. It was the end of February 1944. Early morning. The ground was frozen, and they put a press on the Russians, who still hadn't sobered up from the night before. They were playing for a case of horse dung brandy. Up to the end of the first half, when the first Russian flew into the air, they hadn't realized they were playing in a mine field. But at half time, while the poor guy was taken away to have his leg amputated and arteries tied off, they began boozing it up on that shit-brandy along with the Russians, and they got so drunk that when some Russian captain blew his whistle they all ran onto the field again. Every last one of them. Besides, it was war. They were used to it. It warmed up, the ground softened, it could have exploded under one of them any second. Mungos' old man supposedly felt as if it was all a dream, something surreal. Never in his life had he dribbled like he did that day. He'd passed through the Russian defense like they were made of wax. The end result was six to one. None of them had flown into the air. It seemed it had been some forgotten mine, or else God had been so impressed by their play he'd decided to spare their legs. It was magnificent. Every member of that Russian unit had perished in the spring, at Batina Skela, trying to break through on the Srijem front.

After Mungos finished there was silence. All of us stared at him suspiciously, trying to decide if he'd made it all up. Then he said, "What are you looking at! The message is clear. We have to play like it's a matter of life and death!"

With those words in our heads, we ran onto the field. The Vultures grouped in front of their goal, it was obvious they were going to defend themselves, save the score. So we'd be attacking in waves, like in that mine field. We ran all over, passing, dribbling, shooting. No one was selfish. All of us suddenly felt united, as if anti-infantry mines were under us, or those anti-tank mines that only explode when you jump on them, not with just a tap. It was 1992. In nice weather, when the wind blew from the coast, the rumbling of the heavy artillery from the Velebit Mountains could be heard in the morning silence.

But despite our unity, the ball just didn't want to go into the Vultures' net. It hit the posts or deflected off the goalkeepers' hands, like in a pinball game. Clearly luck was not on our side. At the very moment I thought this the game somehow came to a standstill. I saw our players stop and stare at something by our bench. Even Tomo, who had the ball, stopped at the edge of their penalty box. As if the anthem had sounded suddenly in the middle of our attack.

In front of the bench, completely alone, in Adidas shorts and a T-shirt with the earth printed on it, Globus was standing. Ready to come onto the field. He hopped a little, warming up, and the rest of us stood there. The Cres team didn't move either, everybody at ten hut, like an honor guard. After three days the bereaved had been resurrected, though not the deceased. He'd chosen the most important match for his rebirth. A sharp whistle sounded, and Globus ran onto the field. Slowly, with dignity. As he ran by me he said, "I couldn't look at that fruit anymore!"

We played on with unearthly optimism. Suddenly, we could do whatever we wanted. In the first ten minutes we scored two goals. And luck suddenly came our way. The score was tied, Globus organized our attacks. All of us looked for signs of grief in his play, but there were none. He handled and stopped the ball like in the old days. Perhaps someone could have detected a little sadness in his headshots. I don't know, but when he ran bent forward with his head down, I thought I made out something like grief in his strides. Otherwise, he stopped the ball on his chest, passed it to the tip of his foot with enviable skill, transforming the stop into a deadly shot within a tenth of a second.

That morning Globus demonstrated his true human greatness, like some ancient king or general. He led the island team across the imaginary minefield to a magnificent 4-3 victory. As we went toward the locker room, we heard shots coming from town. Somebody was firing a heckler in honor of our victory. Just then a thunderous boom responded like an echo from the Velebit.

In the locker room, while we took our showers, all of us finally realized we couldn't escape the sadness. Standing in the showers, dripping wet and naked, Globus began to cry. All of a sudden we all got quiet, the murmur of conversation stopped. Only the hum of the showers could be heard. We all pretended to be doing something. We soaped ourselves, plucked hair, gathered our clothes. We didn't want to look at the huge man with the shaved head whining like a little baby.

Mungos suddenly whispered to me, "Look! No hair."

Globus was completely shaved down there. It was weird looking at the genitals of a crying man, even weirder that he hadn't a single hair in his private parts, as if he'd been exposed to radiation. Even his legs were shaved. Clean shaven above and below, with a crying face somewhere in the middle. He had no hair on his chest either. Why did a man whose daughter had died a few days before scrape himself so thoroughly? I couldn't decide if it was sad or just bizarre.

The town with four church towers has as many noons as sides of the world: the bells are not synchronized. St. Andrew always begins first in the dignified baritone of the massive Venetian bronze, which even through five wars was never melted down into cannon balls. A minute later a second noon is sounded by the apple-shaped tower of St. Justine, and later still the third and fourth noons are heard from the cathedral and St. John the Evangelist's. If you were to set up a duel in this town, you wouldn't even get killed on time.

Right after that fourth noon we climbed the shady stairs to the terrace of the Hotel Imperial, the victors just out from their shower, our sports bags on our shoulders. In the hotel bar window our eyes landed on the posters that, as in the old days, announced the visits of traveling entertainers. One advertised a performance by Marcus the magician. There was also a photograph of a woman in a long wooden box being cut in two by a man in a tuxedo. The woman was smiling, but she had already been split, which created a shocking effect. At the bottom of the poster, under the photograph, there was a sign,

> *I cut women in two pieces,*
> *Belly, legs and white tights.*
> *I cut bodies with a sharp saw.*
> *In the end they come out nice.*

The atmosphere around the Tanzplatz and in the shade of the century-old pines was solemn, as if we'd just come down from a funeral, not up from an important victory. In silence the guys took a table next to a white stone balustrade that was a perfect fit for this old Habsburg hotel built under Empress Maria Theresa.

"And the dead people's doctor will sit here!" Muki said patting my shoulder energetically. Somebody had set up a chair there—at the corner of the imperial table—and it seemed it'd been waiting for me for years.

"Pathologist," I said. "That's pathologist!" I tried even though I knew there was no point.

I saw that Maskarin, who seated himself next to me, was trying to tell me something. He leaned conspiratorially toward me and was just waiting for the server who'd come to get our orders to leave before beginning his confession.

He ordered cold wine with water for himself and me, and said, "You know, Fero, I think my wife pees on my food!"

He went on, answering the unstated question in my eyes. "Every lunch smacks of pee: the kale and chard and the chicken stew. It all smells of pee. Not a lot. As if she went in some bigger pot and then just took two or three teaspoons of it out."

Mungos indicated Maskarin with his head and said, "Fero, is he bothering you with his pee stories?"

"I'm not bothering him," said Maskarin nervously, as if Mungos had interrupted a plan. "I thought Fero might take what's left of that potato salad I had for lunch today and have it analyzed."

"Piranha on his mind, not pee," said Tomo. "He's screwing that kid from the store, so he's waiting on his wife's revenge."

"We should console him," said the coach, an expert at soccer and a layman in psychology. "That one would spill a pot of boiling water on you while you're sleeping before she'd pee in your soup."

"So Fero," said Mungos, adding wine to the mix in my glass to strengthen it, "How long has it been?"

I counted on my fingers but couldn't come up with the number. One hand wasn't enough, two were probably too many. Loud laughter suddenly came over from the small group at the next table, unseasonable tourists in heated discussion.

"Journalists," said Tomo, noticing the surprise on my face. "They write about the war in Lika. And they come here because of that bastard."

"Fero doesn't know," said Maskarin. "We're getting famous. An unidentified animal was seen in Dundo. Some kind of a big lizard. There's even a picture in the *Bild Zeitung.*"

"I really want to know, why the photos of those bastards are always blurry?" Tomo said suspiciously.

"Because they're not real," said Maskarin. "Flying saucers either."

But Mungos was quiet and you could tell that something about the animal bothered him. Muki mentioned his grandma, who'd supposedly seen the huge bastard swallow a lamb. Even I remembered those stories about the biggest island forest and sheep disappearing mysteriously.

Meanwhile, one by one the soccer players left, making way for the tourists who took their places at the tables on the terrace. I was surprised to see they were mostly quite fat. I couldn't remember ever seeing such a concentration of fat in one place. A fat symposium. I blurted it out in front of the waiter, who brought me another glass of Babić. This one was free, on the house, for little Mirna in the heavenly soccer fields.

"It's health tourism, sir," said the waiter, indicating the fat people. "Their diet is proscribed, but everything comes down to the fact that we don't give them much."

"Whatcha gonna do, Fero buddy, these last few years, we've sunk low indeed," said Maskarin. "No more normal tourists, just faggots or fatties. If they're neither, they're Czechs."

"They drink mineral water," added Tomo angrily, "and eat French fries, and I throw the fish away, back into the sea, and look at this prick, this magician." Tomo pointed at the poster with a woman cut in half angrily and went on. "Kićo and Tereza used to sing here before, and now this jerk is cutting a chick on the terrace, and he cuts the same chick every evening and she's so drunk she hardly makes it into the box."

"Not even the lizard can help us," added the coach, resigned.

"I need you!" whispered Mungos suddenly. He was serious, which was unexpected. "I want you too see something."

He stood up just then and gave my shoulder a discrete tap, which I guess meant I was supposed to follow. We said goodbye to the soccer players and tourist analysts, who would soon be moving on to politics and the detonations audible from the Velebit.

On the stairs Mungos hugged me like an old friend, and we started toward town, his arm around my shoulder. His behavior was rather mysterious. The ornaments on the tiles we walked on resembled some children's drawings from Auschwitz that I'd had the opportunity of seeing in one of the synagogues in Prague. They were completely new and bright, like hard snow. And they screeched under our feet.

"This is new, isn't it?" I said.

Yes," said Mungos. "It's from Goli Otok. Old stock. When they closed down the penitentiary, they found this in the warehouses. They forced the inmates to break stone and make tiles."

"That's why they cry!" I said. As if that explained anything.

When we reached the Hotel Istria, we turned right toward the old wine cellar. In the lobby, which used to be a tourist agency, the reception desk was torn down and everything smelled of urine. The parquet tiles had been removed from the concrete floor and placed in the corner next to sacks of sand.

It was obvious that work had stopped suddenly, in the middle of remodeling. An obese rat ran in front of us and disappeared somewhere behind the piled up construction material. It was the size of a small cat. I tried to figure how many times you would have to spit on meeting such a big ass rat to keep bad luck away.

We made our way downstairs. I felt cold air coming from somewhere. We descended for quite a while down the semicircular metal stairs, at the bottom of which stretched the largest wine cellar on the island — a couple of large underground rooms. Only the first room we entered was lit by a weak lamp hanging down from the ceiling. The brick arches and sour, heavy air reminded me of when I used to buy wine here as a kid, before Christmas and Easter, and then take the heavy demijohns home tied on my scooter. All around were shelves with dusty bottles without labels. The puffs of air that came from the dark rooms made the cobwebs on the half-vaulted ceiling quiver.

Mungos stopped, listening, and then yelled into the dark, "Thief! You're drinking again!"

First we heard the sound of rubber soles on the old ceramic floor, like the squeaking of the door in a horror movie. Then a man in a police uniform appeared carrying an open bottle in his hand.

"The glasses are there," he said, pointing at a barrel that was tipped flat.

Mungos introduced me, and I shook hands with the policeman. "Fero's one of the Pipici family." His hand was cold and moist. We each had a glass of Rizvanac, swirling it in our mouths like experts.

Then Mungos said, "Bring her in now! For Fero to see!"

The policeman disappeared into one of the dark rooms.

When he came back he was pushing a gurney with a body covered with a white sheet in front of him. There was blood on the fabric around the head in irregular stains that reminded me of modern art. At that moment the policeman's Motorola crackled and his hand went to his waist. Somebody needed to talk to Mungos, and they retreated into the next room. The conversation was obviously confidential and about the corpse on the gurney. I watched the gurney and the dead body on it in the semi-darkness, aware that it would need to be pushed right under the lamp for me to really see anything.

But then the thing on the stretcher moved. I saw the sheet rising around the stomach and then slowly lower. I had a very bad feeling about this. I was used to dead bodies from my job, but I wasn't too pleased about corpses that moved.

"Your body's moving," I muttered when the policeman and Mungos came back. Something in my throat prevented me from saying it more distinctly.

"Eh! Bullshit," said Mungos, writing down something he had evidently been told over the radio. "You'd better take a look."

The policeman removed the sheet at last. He did it routinely and theatrically like magicians when they take sheets from the women they've just sawed in half or stabbed with their swords. The movement made a small rat, which had been crawling over the body under the sheet, run away. The body, I had to admit, wasn't moving. It showed clear signs of stiffness. It was naked and female, with huge breasts that had sagged down and moved apart and then stiffened. There was a nasty open wound on her neck, full of deep bruises and curdled blood, but it was clear she'd been pretty and quite young. The problem appeared lower, below the stomach. It was a medium sized male penis and testicles along with it.

"Dick's bigger than Muki's," said the policeman. "And she's a woman?"

"Let me introduce you," said Mungos. "This is the Little Match Girl. They called her that because she'd been spreading the drip around. The sting must have reminded them of that. Matches."

I confess it was the most beautiful specimen of a transsexual I'd ever met on the autopsy table. Or rather, on a facsimile of an autopsy table.

"Why here," I asked, "when you have a mortuary and fridges up there? I remember when it was built, from the referendum."

Mungos looked at me as if the question surprised him. "You know the people around here and still ask that? Rumors started spreading right off when we found her. People collected in front of the mortuary and refused to let the girl with the dick be put in with their dead. Probably afraid she might contaminate them."

"The council president told us to put her somewhere cool, just not in the mortuary," added the policeman, the whole time looking with disgust at that prick.

"Her name's Marillena," said Mungos. "She worked at the strip club on Palit. At Stipe's. I wanted to show you before we send her on to Rijeka for the autopsy."

"Where did you find her? Or him?" I felt compelled to make the point.

"Near the campground," said the policeman. "This morning around nine."

Her neck was literally all chewed up.

"What could have caused such a wound?"

"I don't know," I said and stared at the roll of flesh and curdled blood. At first sight, the wound was strange—deep tooth cuts in combination with relatively shallow bites.

"I've never seen anything like it," I said. "The tissue needs to be analyzed, and everything else."

"That's what I was afraid of," said Mungos. "Could a saw have done this?"

"Theoretically, yes, but not likely. It looks like teeth to me."

"There's no animal around here that could do that," the policeman said. "Except for a shark, but that's in water."

"We're fucked," said Mungos.

After we'd put the corpse away, Mungos and I went to the town boardwalk. A breeze was gently rocking the boats. Some twenty years before we'd used to meet here, in front of the Hotel Istria, as soon as the town had been plunged into dark. Then Mungos would say, "Hey, guys! Let's go beat up some faggots!"

What a pleasant memory to have.

3 FRANKA

There were fewer and fewer people on the island to visit, and even those still living, as a poet once said, did so only temporarily. Life got more temporary all the time. That was the story with Franka, a friend who worked at the island's only library. She was thirty-six, a virgin, had breast cancer, and was into horoscopes, though not professionally. I stopped by to say hello. It was close to one o'clock, the end of the library's working hours on Sunday.

We greeted each other like friends, a little kiss on the cheek, then she wiped the traces of her make up from my face with a hanky after wetting it with saliva.

"Don't worry!" she said. "I'm not contagious."

Some tiny old man came to return his books. Franka examined them carefully. After she'd made certain everything was all right, she put them on the shelves.

"It's not what you think," she said, noticing my surprised look. "This isn't some old maid's whim. We're looking for a guy who's defacing our books."

"Ah-hah! He must be a dangerous criminal."

"He borrows books and rips the ends out. You read a detective story and there's no end, the resolution's missing. Instead the pervert writes something like 'This book's ending is cancelled' or 'A message from Franz Kafka.'"

"Can't you get him by his handwriting? Hand out a query to every patron or something."

"We've tried that, but he changes his writing. He even got a children's printing press so now he's printing his messages."

"Troublesome type," I pronounced, not knowing what else to say. I looked at her thin arms and fragile shoulders and felt sad, thinking she wouldn't last long.

"Lately he's become more perfidious. He noticed we were examining every book. So now the swine destroys the beginning. He prints in capital letters in red ink on the second or third page, 'The killer is Theresa Arundell' or 'Miss Lawson's terrier discovers the murderer, it's Charles Arundell, the playboy.' We came up with a countermeasure, though. We put a white sticker over his message to save the book at least for a while. But the guy's tireless. He puts a stamp over the sticker, 'Fuck you! The murderer is still Charles Arundell.'"

"If you want, I'll help you catch this bastard before he destroys the bulk of your most read stuff."

By the end of the shortened Sunday working hours, a man whose face I rememberd from somewhere came in — grizzled beard, glasses, shiny bald head with what was left of his hair combed to the back. An intellectual. Franka greeted him warmly, like a valued customer.

"Miss Franka, have you ever eaten birds?" asked the man. "I don't mean chickens, turkeys and such, but real birds, the ones that fly."

"I don't remember," said Franka, giggling, and he emptied the books out of his plastic bag onto the counter.

"There's one book here. It's called Birds. Just like that, Birds. I checked it with the plumb, it's okay to read it."

She took the books, put the cards back in without checking the number of pages and put them back on the shelf.

"It's all in the bones, I'm telling you. That's why they can fly."

"I'm not for those gourmand thingies," said Franka. The smile wouldn't leave her face, she liked this guy so much.

"Would you like to browse a little?" she asked, her affection palpable.

"No, not now," he said. "I can see you have company today, some other time. *Adio!*" He folded his bag and disappeared through the door without looking at me once, as if I were made of air.

"Is he from Kampor as well?" I asked.

"What Kampor?" Franka replied. "What are you talking about?"

"From the nut house. He talks like it."

"Oh no. He's imitating Ranko. He handles the plumb. People around the island say he isn't crazy, but he's trying to get a pension for being disabled."

"Why haven't you checked his books?"

"He doesn't borrow novels," she said. "He's looking after some old bed-ridden woman. He reads children's stories to her before she goes to sleep. That's the only thing she still understands. Otherwise he writes novels. He was even popular for a while. We read him at school."

"That's why I recognized his face," I said. "From the book covers. Beard, glasses, bald head."

After the bearded man had gone, Franka locked the door and pulled the Venetian blinds on the windows so the sun, when it grew hot, wouldn't damage the books.

"I think you're buying me lunch," she said. "I'm not hungry often. You have to take advantage of this."

We found a table in the main room at the Sunčani Sat, "The Sundial," the place with the shark on the wall. A fine sight. At the tables people ate fish, on the wall a people-eating fish. It was a shark that had been caught in the town harbor at the end of the summer of '78. The Franciscans from St. Euphemia stuffed it, and a previous owner hung the monster on the wall as a decoration and a warning for the guests: eat or you'll be eaten. Universal reciprocity, just like in Shakespeare. People said a men's size ten loafer had been found in the monster's stomach. Under the beast, in a couple of languages, there was a sign that read, "Enjoy your meal!"

Franka has an excellent appetite. She digs into her sea bass like it's the shark that ate the family she never had. We hadn't finished half our meal when Maskarin showed up at our table.

"So you're gorging yourself on expensive fish, eh?" he says, pulling up the chair from the next table. "Don't let me bother you. I'm just passing by."

"Want some?" I ask, polite. I know he can't afford sea bass. His children cost a lot of money, his alimony too. All of his lawyer income is spent on pencil cases and slippers. Besides, people around here don't sue each other much, there aren't many trials, and property boundaries are made of rocks.

"No thanks," he says. "I already had lunch. But I'll take

some Postup." He's already pouring himself a glass of the dark red blood.

"You haven't returned the books!" Franka says harshly, between two bites.

"I told my kids to bring them back, but you know them. I'll return them one of these days."

He turns back to me, "So how are things up there?"

"Not good," I say. "My wife left me, we're divorced."

"Did she take a lot?"

"He doesn't look at it like that," Franka interrupts again, taking out one especially long sea bass rib and licking it. She enjoys it as if it's Adam's.

Maskarin sees he's gone too far by bringing up money so he goes back to the old days, trying to camouflage the second glass he's pouring for himself. Postup's the most expensive wine you can get here.

"Do you remember the crying game in Zagreb, at Gumica? Back then we had a future. Now I often catch myself in front of the mirror in my office, asking if this is the future."

"For a beer, he could make a stone curb at the bus station cry," I say, and explain the game we played during our studies to Franka. "When we'd get to Gumica, sometime after a long night, Maskarin would tell me, 'I bet you a beer I can make that jerk by the window cry.' There he is, some poor guy standing next to the window, sucking on his brandy and soda. His face hasn't seen a razor in a while, his shoes are out of fashion and all muddy, his pants are canvas. Probably a construction worker passing through. Maskarin takes his beer and approaches. 'Can I sit with you for a while, buddy,' he says, and then unleashes his story. He has a sister, his only relative in the world, but the poor thing went mad. She graduated early, and then something happened to her brain and she went nuts. Once, on Kvatrić

Square, he says, he saw a good piece of ass in skin tight jeans. He followed the ass and got a hard on. What could he do, he's a man. He hears the Albanian hawkers whistling after the ass as it moves flirtatiously. It floated between the wax beans and lemons as if it wasn't walking on earth. And then he recognized her. His sister! He'd got a hard on for his own sister, the poor crazy thing in her exotic clothes and colorful wigs."

"And that makes them cry?" Franka asks in disbelief.

"Sometimes," I say. "They've got a lot of misery of their own, so all they need is just a little nudge. Still, if that story doesn't work, he's got another."

Meanwhile, Maskarin finished the bottle of Postup and moved on to picking at what was left of our sea bass.

"Do you want them to bring you a plate?" asks Franka generously, without any irony, and Makarin gets defensive. He doesn't want to eat, he just wants to taste a little to see if they prepared it well.

"The other story is even sadder. He says he's got a little girl he loves more than anything in the world. No father loves his daughter more. The kid's smart, she'd even be pretty if she didn't have a big dark purple spot on her left cheek. Like a burn. And so, he was once with that little girl of his in the park where he caught sight of a pair of exceptional boobs. With good boobs of course go good legs. Naked ones since it's spring. The left leg under the left boob and the right one under the right boob. Each boob has its own leg, and the face isn't bad either. He starts a conversation with those boobs and legs. She's a student. And when his little girl comes out with something like, 'Daddy, look at me. I'm on the merry go round,' he pretends he's not *that* daddy. And what for? For some pussy! The worker passing through is already bawling, his tears drop into his brandy and soda. Maskarin pretends he's shedding a tear with him too, just a little, for company's sake, and then he winks at me. 'Get the beer,' he says."

"You're sick! I don't like this."

"She doesn't know the most important part," says Maskarin, with a mysterious grin.

"Both stories are *true*," I deliver the kicker. "The kid's his daughter from his first marriage up in Zagreb. There's something wrong with the capillaries in her face. And his sister, as you know, is in Kampor."

A moment of silence. Franka needs some time to put all these things together, and then a little dark cloud with lightning and little stars forms above her head.

"Excuse me for a moment," says Maskarin, as if he's seen the lightning and little clouds, and goes slowly toward the restroom. Franka accepts his departure with relief. She leans toward me over the mortal remains of the fish and says, "I don't like him. Besides, I think he's suspect."

"What makes you think that?" I can't imagine Maskarin engaged into ripping up books. It doesn't fit.

"I don't know. No particular reason. Intuition maybe."

4 THE CLINIC

I'm awakened from my afternoon nap by a gentle piano tune being played by a little girl from the neighborhood, whose mother died of leukemia. It's Sunday. Six o'clock in the afternoon. One of those moments when the clock on the wall looks like a compass. The minute hand points up and the hour hand down. Like some kind of dilemma. Or the need to make a decision. I don't like it when clocks warn me of things.

I'm lying in the huge bed that belonged to my parents, also dead, and I'm thinking about the Match Girl. Dead. All in all, I'm surrounded by dead people in this quite pleasant moment as a variety of sounds melt into the piano passage. The yelling from the beach is replaced by sea gull calls, and the buzzing of skimmers gives way to the clatter of fishing boats. The fall, I see, is here. It comes in these tiny, unimportant things.

Then the phone in the living room rings. I wait for a moment, and when I realize there's no one to pick it up because I'm the only one still alive in the house, I rush downstairs. It's Mungos.

"I made arrangements with the doctor," he says. "She's waiting for us at her office."

Ten minutes later we're on our way down to the boardwalk from which we'll proceed to the health center on the other side of the bay, between the soccer field and the gas station. At the Istria, however, we run into a beggar. He has a very odd look. He's wearing a good suit with a bow-tie, like a lawyer's, only everything's extremely dirty. His pants are shiny with grease around his knees, as if they're made of leather.

"It's Beno," Mungos says. "From 'Benign.' They call him that because he works in front of the Rijeka Hospital. He shakes hands with the patients who come out of Oncology. They're worried, they've been examined. They're thinking the worst. Then he tells them, 'God bless you, you don't have cancer. It's just mastopathy. It's benign! Spare a quarter? It's benign, not dangerous.' He looks them right in the eye, as if telling their fortune. No wonder he makes more than any other beggar. The elite of scroungers."

Beno sees Mungos, and, pretending to be completely indifferent, changes his position to slink strategically away between the wall and a parked Opel. But Mungos' police voice thunders, "Beno! Come here!"

Caught, the aristocratic scrounger now crosses the boardwalk reluctantly and comes to our side, the side of the law.

"So, Beno, here you are again, eh?" Mungos begins his detective conversation. "What, Rijeka's no good anymore?"

"I came to look at my late father's grave a little," Beno says, playing on our sentiments. He can't do anything but look. First, because he doesn't have any money for flowers and candles, and second, because he sold the grave to someone else long ago, so now somebody else lies in it, and his father's name is on the back of the gravestone, as are the names of all the others sold by their relatives. Mungos explains all this to me in short, and now I remember Beno. We went to school together. He was a couple of years older than us and used to fillip us on the heads.

Mungos spat the police truth into his face: "You came here because you saw there are sick people around. You're attracted by this health tourism thing. Tachycardias, heart-attacks, patients for Beno the Vulture. People tell me they saw you at Škver near the heart clinic?"

"No, I wasn't there, Jesus my witness!" Beno whimpers, seeing there's no joking with the devil. Mungos and joking—definitely not a good combination. "You know I don't work here!" the aristocrat rolls out his last argument—the truth—directly into Mungos' face. They're like two professionals.

Mungos gave him a hug and an okay-I'll-let-you-go-this-time look, as if he'd forgiven him something just awful, and the three of us promenaded before the parked boats and their owners. Beno's face was discomfited: the chief of police had his arm around him, a beggar, in public, while the boat farers, who usually screwed around with him, looked on with contempt.

Stinking spy, he's ratting somebody again," commented a relative of Muki's, a little smarter and with a longer dick.

But Beno was wrenched in and couldn't escape the law's iron embrace.

After we'd walked some ways from the boat owners, Mungos squeezed him hard and said, "Don't bullshit me! Tell me what's going on!"

I was to one side like some witness to the Inquisition, listening to their conversation.

"There's something strange at the friars' place," Beno answers, all business. "You know I eat there. New friars have come, and they won't let me in anymore. Inside the monastery. The new ones have taken control of everything."

But Mungos is visibly angry. "What's this bullshit about friars? What are you talking about?"

"I'm just saying," says Beno, aware that he's gaining an advantage, "they've got suvs. What are friars doing with suvs?"

Mungos pauses, surprised. First, the friar who'd spoken at Mirna's funeral wasn't from the island. He didn't even know the kid's name. He'd had to read it from a piece of paper. And now a reliable informant, though unreliable man, was talking about some Franciscan suvs. He let Beno go, pondering. His face showed he was thinking about the odd friars and out of place suvs, and nothing was clear. Just as it wasn't clear to me why the police chief my former friend was dragging me around on his investigation.

He turned toward the clinic and I followed. There, in the pleasant cool of an empty waiting room—it was Sunday and the doctor's office was closed—I, the doctor for the dead, met the doctor for the living, and in my humble opinion, she could have brought many to back life with her abundant protrusions. She was filling in for Renata, who was taking her funeral days off. We chatted, but Mungos was all business. He was going through the patients' records. I saw he'd even taken Muki's file out.

"Is he a suspect too?"

"No," says Mungos, "but I have to take him into consideration because he's dripping. The poor guy had a birthday. The boys met under Marijan to play cards, when somebody says, 'Hey, Muki's already forty, and he still hasn't fucked.' They decide to collect some money and give him something for his birthday. Tomo took the thing over and introduced Marillena to Muki as a joke. A few days after, it started to burn when he peed. The matches were lit. The day after, the whole island knew. They yelled behind him in the street: 'First time with a guy?!' And his dick is so small, Renata hardly managed to take a swab in her office."

While Mungos explained the genesis of Muki's gonorrhea, I couldn't get the sad picture out of my head: I see Renata holding that little midget Muki's wiener in her hand, searching for the tiny hole with the gauze. At just that moment, she remembers her dying daughter. And begins to weep. Muki's embarrassed. He sees the doctor crying and his dick retreats even deeper into that Balzac fat of his. Renata's crying her heart out, her tears drop onto Muki's testicles. The poor thing's losing her child and here she is handling some tiny gonorrheal dick.

"Here's another one!" yells the intern somewhere from the other office, bringing a file.

"There are tourists' records," she explains and hands the file to Mungos.

He looks at the name and says, "That's what we were looking for!"

I see the name, actually the pseudonym, of the magician

who cuts women in half on hotel terraces, scribbled in marker ink on the edge of the cardboard flap of the doctor's file.

"The saw master," Mungos says emphatically.

"Who else is there?" I say, as if we've actually got someone and as if this concerns me.

"Ranko, from the Pipići's," says Mungos. "He's also been raving about saws. Then Ratko Cvrle, he's bi, he'll stuff it up anyone, then Stipe Tovarina, who owns the night club. She worked for him."

"All studs you mean! But in fact all fags," I say, opening the office door, when Mungos' suspicious look in the direction of the waiting room shuts me up. Suddenly the waiting room has filled with people. Locals, old grannies and grandpas, have noticed the doctor's open office, so they forget it's Sunday and are now waiting for the big-breasted angel to write them prescriptions for drugs that most likely won't help anyway.

The two of us, rather distracted, leave the waiting room without noticing the phantom who probably stole out just then and hurried after us across the soccer field. The freak approaches us from behind.

"Did you know," he says, "that little Mirna was raped in the mortuary?"

It's Ranko. He's got gonorrhea too. It seems he's been following us and now plays some absurd game.

"First they took her out. While they were taking her out, one of the jerks drooled all over her, God rest her soul, and his dribbles dropped on the kid's shirt. Then the other one came and spread her legs with the Volkswagen jack. That made her stockings tear. She was probably stiff…"

"Ugh, stop bullshitting," says Mungos, seemingly cool.

"I'm not! They did it! Fucking tree beachers!"

"They who?" I ask. I'm very curious.

"Them. The friars! They all took turns fucking that poor little girl…"

Mungos suddenly turned and grabbed the Franciscan theorist by his shirt. "You pedophilic prick," yelled the chief. "I have a paper here with your name on it. It says that pus is dripping from your dick. That means you fucked that freak up the ass. Maybe later you opened her neck with that saw of yours…"

"I'm not lying," says Ranko, stretched on his toes because Mungos is holding him a little above ground. "Ask my late mother… I keep her in the fridge. Sardines and chicken make her go, because not everybody needs a body when nature calls."

Mungos lets him go, and Ranko lands safely on the ground. Now he follows stepping firmly on the soccer grass, but his mind is still in the clouds. At least that's how it seems.

"My ma like all ma's is always bull-shitting about something. My son, how can you keep your mother in the fridge? Still better that than an old folk's home. She lives on the door with a bottle of coke and a jar of mustard, and at night she shakes the fridge and wakes me up."

We reached the marina and the yacht jetty. Ranko's still hopping after us. I confess we're not sure what he's up to. Then, without turning back, Mungos makes things plain: "I know you're pretending because of your disability pension. You don't have to screw around with me because of it. I won't rat you out to the disability board. But a murder is different, and I'll bust your balls for that, though I don't give a fuck about that Romanian creep. Got it?!"

Ranko paused and smiled as if he'd understood. And now he just stands on the shore and giggles with that you-can't-touch-me smile on his face.

"My ma loves you so much!" he says instead of goodbye.

46

We go on toward the police station. It's a warm early fall evening and the sea breeze wrinkles the harbor's water, which is darker, the colors clearer. In my youth, when it seemed most things still made sense, this was my favorite time, the ripeness of the summer gliding into fall.

"Where are we going?" I ask, just to break the silence, unbearable after Ranko.

5 THE SECRET OF OLD JADREŠIN'S STENCH

"To see Maskarin. Then we'll have some fun with the saw master," says Mungos as we pass the police station. "He has to be dented a little, psychologically I mean, if we want to get anything out of him."

I know the saw master only from the poster on the Hotel Imperial window, but I really want to see what dirty trick Mungos is planning that made him so cheerful all of a sudden. And it's dirty tricks that make Mungos happy, for as long as I can remember, ever since we were kids. And, when I think of it, it was actually Mungos who put an end to my childhood, on the day I learned why Old Jadrešin's hands smelled so bad.

At the end of my sophomore year, after my mother died, and my father got a job on Goli Otok, we settled on this island town where we used to spend our summers. We had no one to cook for us, so we took out a meal credit with Old Jadrešin, who ran a kind of a tavern for the locals. He cooked our breakfast and lunch, and we prepared our dinner ourselves, in the candle light, thinking about Mother. Old Jadrešin made excellent omelets, poached eggs, sautéed cuttlefish in wine with rosemary. But his hands stank all the time.

47

My old man said it was because Old Jadrešin was a fisherman. As if all men around here were not fishermen, but their hands didn't stink like that. I can still call to mind that smell, which penetrated straight into my brain, some mixture of rotten fish and solvent: organic decay and chemical dilution. As if he was always cleansing his hands of something with a solvent. Old Jadrešin had prepared our lunch for about a year when I noticed his hands sometimes smelled and sometimes didn't. Actually, I didn't know when they smelled and when they didn't. Maybe they smelled all the time even when I thought they didn't but I just couldn't smell it. Also I noticed they smelled more when St. Andrew was ringing. I couldn't figure out why.

Then Mungos took us to see how they buried the American. A man from the island who had died in Pittsburgh, and had now found his repose here, among the rocks, because that's where he'd been born at the end of the last century. We hid behind the graves of the Sisters of Mercy and other island aristocracy, in the main alley, where a nice view opened on the lower, plebeian part of the cemetery. There was a great black marble tomb, which had been nationalized after the war, and in the sixties the town council gave it up for the Americans to be buried in, as a sign of gratitude because the emigrant community had given the money for the restoration of the town walls. That's why every five to ten feet a different name was chiseled into the wall: Vjeko Španjol, Matija Beg, Sino Krstinić, Dominik Ribarić.

We lay on the warm grave of the Sisters of Mercy. It was as if not the sun above, but their bodies below were warming the stone, beneath which there was nothing but a couple of stiff calcium formations and dust.

The squeak of the un-greased hinges on the wrought iron gates signaled the American's entrance into the holy cemetery ground. A small group with the priest in front went in, but neither the funeral music nor the procession of the grieving followed. Behind the consecrated character with the prayer book in his hands they pushed a gurney with a chest on it. We were shocked.

"Jesus! Not even my cat would fit into that," Muki said. The coffin was unnaturally small. The chest was actually about one third of a regular man's size in length and a little more than that in width. Like an unwieldy suitcase.

"Was this American a dwarf?" I asked, my voice hoarse.

"No, he wasn't a dwarf," Mungos said. "They cut them!"

"Cut them?"

"Yeah, when they die, there in America," Mungos went on, "they ship or fly a coffin here, and then one of our people from the island cuts them in half. Then they put them in square boxes like this so they're easier to stack into the grave. They can fit more of them in the council tomb. And no other tomb needs to be nationalized."

We were silent meanwhile. Each of us pictured the American cut in half, and the images were obviously quite unpleasant. When they lowered the short chest into the open tomb, down in the town St Andrew's bells sounded the solemn tune for the dead.

"No one knows who cuts them," Mungos said. "But somebody's in charge of it. He has some other occupation, moves around in society, a respectable member of the community."

Next morning, while Old Jadrešin was preparing our omelet I realized I'd discovered the secret of his hands' stench. I'd somehow grown up with it. My father, a prison psychiatrist, who knew well how everything actually went in life, and I sat at the table and ate the excellent omelet that Old Jadrešin had prepared for us with his stinky hands. Like two adults.

Afterwards Mungos claimed Old Jadrešin cut Americans for other islands too: Susak, Cres, Pag, Lošinj. That is, they cut them up on those islands too. It was the usual practice with dead Americans on the Karst terrain. Supposedly Old Jadrešin had cut up all the dead Americans in the whole Kvarner, but his eggs were still as good as they get. A miracle or what?

6 THE FRAME-UP

Maskarin sits with his feet on the desk in the shade of his law office. This probably gives him the feeling that everything around him is America. Mungos and I have made ourselves relatively comfortable on the other side of the desk, the one for clients, and we spin around in our chairs like little kids. We test the hydraulics and rotation. Everything's quiet while Maskarin ponders whether to take part in our joint frame-up of the saw master.

"You don't have to chip in," Mungos says, not wanting to scare him away. "Fero and I will pay, you just hand him our dough."

"Why me?" says Maskarin, as if Mungos is trying to get him into some dangerous scheme.

"Because I'm the police chief. That's why. Have you ever seen the authorities screwing around with the public? Anyway you don't give a fuck, you're not in the public service."

Maskarin thinks again, then says, "Fero, do you know how our friend became the chief of the police?"

"Don't listen to him! He's full of shit!"

"He worked in the administration down there at the po-lice station, and when the new government arrived, they see 'arrested for nationalist chauvinism' in his file. Fifteen years ago they caught him playing with himself on Frkanje, above the nudist beach. They wanted to let him go, but when they asked him who he jerked off on and told him he'd better answer, he blabbered the Velebit Fairy. He stayed in the poky for three days and got a file with a flag, which is what they called the special note. For chauvinism and western propaganda."

"Fero's not crazy enough to trust a lawyer," Mungos said.

"And who's he going to trust? The police?"

Trusting any of them was the furthest thing from my mind. I was thinking hard about who was in charge of sawing today. Because there were still Americans here, and more important they were dying more than ever and the council tomb probably hadn't grown any bigger. It wasn't like a female reproductive organ to develop its capacities over time.

But Mungos says, "The commies even hated the Maestral because it blows from the west."

"But the Velebit Fairy isn't from the west, right?!" says Maskarin. "She's from the north. She's with the north wind, not the Maestral."

Then he pauses, as if he's made a decision, and says, "Let me send this fax and then I'll go down to the boardwalk with you. The magician's at Sutjeska now, having his coffee."

This meant we'd won him over.

We slipped quickly out of Maskarin's office on Srednja Street, above the pharmacy, and went down toward the town's Loggia and the café whose name had been changed long ago, though everybody still called it Sutjeska, probably because the new name was even worse.

Just in front of the café Maskarin stopped. "There he is! Give me the dough and I'll take it to him."

Mungos fished out a bundle of bills from his pocket and

discretely shoved the money into the lawyer's hand. "You know what to say?"

"Fuck, I'm not some kid!"

Maskarin slowly waddled to the table where the saw master was sitting with some woman. Probably the one he sawed in half at hotel terraces every night. I watched him walk. It was definitely the gait of a man whose wife peed in his food. As if ammoniac had more effect on his back than on his stomach.

"Fero, see if he gives him all the dough!" said Mungos, peeking behind the corner like a child.

"Why wouldn't he?" I asked naively.

"When money's in question with him, you gotta be careful."

We moved on toward Palit and the strip club only after I'd convinced Mungos that Maskarin had given the bundle of controversial money to the saw master, putting it into the breast pocket of his shirt. The club was run by the only Primorac on the island with a Bosnian nickname: Stipe Striptiz. The Bosnian construction workers who'd built his business premises gave it to him. Even the club, whose name was actually Aphrodita, people called ss. So whenever the island kids sprayed two big Ss — like Mengele's twins — on the walls with car paint, no one actually knew if they were neo-Nazis or just advertising Stipe's business. As the Little Match Girl had danced her last dance, just before she died, on Stipe's German stainless steel strip poles, a visit to Stipe was Mungos' logical next step. Besides, the frame-up included him too. I just didn't know how.

Red neon letters resembling handwriting glimmered at the entrance into the Aphrodita. But inside there was no striptease: first of all, the daily news that all the employees and rare guests watched with great interest was on TV, and second, the only stripper had been killed not two days before. Stipe greeted us warmly, inviting us from behind the bar to take a seat at two tall bar stools. He looked completely different than he had at the funeral. His long red hair was not tied behind his head, like at the cemetery, but fluttered about loose. And instead of dark sun glasses he wore his old John Lennon glasses which he seldom took off. A hippie striptease entrepreneur.

"Telepathy!" he said to Mungos. "I was just thinking about you."

"I was thinking about you too," said Mungos ironically, climbing onto the bar stool. "You know old hookers shouldn't sit on chairs like this?"

"I know," says Striptiz, pretending to be happy, as if there were no war and his only employee hadn't just violently quit this world. "Because they'll fall through."

"I wonder," says Mungos, playing with the bags of sugar in the ceramic jar on the bar, "about hookers who don't have a pussy? Can they sit on chairs like this?"

Meanwhile he abruptly opens one of the bags, pours a few white crystals onto the back of his hand and licks it.

"Hrvoje, you don't have to fuck around with me like that!" says Striptiz. "I'll tell you all I know."

"You better!" says Mungos. "Fero, try the sugar. Stipe has the best sugar."

While a little further down the bar Stipe pours us two glasses of Karlovačko without asking what we'll have, I whisper, "And what if he refused to cooperate?"

"Then this wouldn't be sugar," says Mungos.

On the TV, the daily news has just shown a truck full of corpses. One of the truck drivers is demonstrating in front of the camera how on one corpse a part of the scull separated from the rest, which meant he'd been killed with a hammer. Or maybe she. It wasn't too clear.

"Fero, you haven't been here a shit load of years," says Striptiz, putting the coasters on the bar out of habit and the glasses of beer on top.

Mungos takes a sip, wipes the foam from his face, and says: "OK, tell me everything you know. Who did she sleep with? What did she do there at the camp? Anything unusual?"

All genuine investigator's questions, I see, as if Mungos isn't just a clerk, but a trained detective. As if we are in fact in the middle of a real investigation and not just killing time until the crime squad from Rijeka arrives.

"Who she slept with or did she sleep with somebody, I don't know," says Stipe. "You know I don't do that stuff. But as for weird... She had somebody...."

"She had more than one like that," says Mungos.

"A serious one."

Silence. Mungos is obviously thinking who on the island could love a Romanian prostitute with a dick.

"She was saving for the operation!" says Striptiz.

It was bizarre but comforting that everybody spoke about Marillena as female.

"She wanted to get married," Stipe added.

"What luck!" Mungos seemed touched. "You have to pay to have it cut off."

"Last year around this time she went away, home to Constanza. I saw something weird was going on."

"Weird?"

"I don't know. She wasn't like before. She had dough."

"Why did she go to Constanza?"

"Her aunt passed away. That's what she said, but I'm not sure if it's true. She had no contacts with relatives. She never got any letters..."

"And who's the serious guy?"

"I don't know. She didn't say."

The pictures on the TV had changed. There were no more corpses. Now it was a map of Croatia with little yellow suns drawn on it. The weather would be nice for the next few days. A couple of those who'd been sitting in the semi-darkness got up and went toward the exit. I could tell they'd come here only to watch the news. Mungos glanced at his watch and finished his beer.

"Want to go with us to the Imperial?" he said. It was immediately obvious the investigation had finished and what followed was informal hanging out. "There's a bottle of Plavac waiting for us up there."

On our way to the hotel terrace we had to pass by the fall tree. It was a thirty year old Canadian maple a sailor had planted here to remind him of the vast Alaskan forests. No one knew how it survived in this climate, completely adjusted to the Mediterranean heat and dryness. The only thing it brought from the north was the genetically inscribed time of losing its leaves. At the beginning of September its leaves, now completely yellow, would fall to the grass under its grayish branches. As kids we used to stop here at the end of the summer to watch the fall.

Up on the terrace Maskarin was already sitting at our table next to the balustrade, sipping his Dingač. One could tell immediately he'd ordered the most expensive wine they had because he wasn't paying. We sat down without a word, and Maskarin placed a glass in front of each of us and poured the dark red fluid into it. The terrace was half-empty. A couple of fat guests in the corner next to the aperitif bar. About a dozen journalists and foreign photographers resting from the front lines, and at a table in front of the stage two pairs of Italian yacht owners who'd come to see what a country at war looked like. That was all the guests there were when the singer of the local band announced the magician. He said the famous Magic Markus was to perform, but instead his assistant appeared in a circus costume before the audience. She circled once around the podium, smiling and waving a handkerchief.

"Drunk again!" said Mungos. He was right. Something in the way she walked told you she had too much alcohol in her. She wasn't tottering, but there was something, an exaggerated enthusiasm. For a while we watched the drunk circling with music in the background. There was something archetypal about her. Then two assistants brought the box. It resembled a white coffin for children, except it didn't have those decorations, and it was square. The woman opened the box and tried to get in, but she almost fell over. One of the assistants had to help her. The music continued to play.

Only after her torso was inside, her head and legs sticking out, did the assistants put everything up on the table. The music stopped and everything got quiet for a moment. Until the magician appeared. We were bewildered to see him in a tailcoat, a white shirt and bow tie, a long reddish wig, and John Lennon glasses. He looked almost exactly like Stipe Striptiz — they even had the same stature.

"What the fuck is this?" says Stipe, his voice raucous, as if he's got sand paper in his vocal cords. I see Mungos smiling, and Maskarin looks at everything with a pinch of fear. He's waiting to see what will happen.

Meanwhile the magician's taken up the saw and shows it to the audience. The drummer's drumming. But just as he makes the first cut, the music stops, and that characteristic sawing sound is audible. At the same time, Stipe's face has turned red. The hotel staff, maids, bartenders, cooks, everybody's standing in the audience and laughing loudly. Franko, the receptionist, tosses in loud enough for everybody to hear, "Striptiz, you're doing geat. So that's how you cut 'em, is it?"

The magician began singing:

I cut corpses in two pieces,
Belly, legs and white tights.
I cut bodies with a sharp saw.
In the end they come out nice.

Stipe's face contorted like that of a man relieving himself after eating a couple pounds of chocolate. Then he moved. He covered those few meters in a second and hit the magician in the face above the box with the woman sawn half through. When the magician staggered back, Stipe knocked down the box and continued beating him. The woman waved her hands and legs, trapped in the wooden frame.

"Fuck you, you faggot motherfucker!" he screamed. "You won't fuck around with me, you gonorrheal piece of shit!"

The magician crouched and the blood from his mouth dripped onto his shiny shoes. Stipe kicked the magician in the head just right, and he hit the ground as if a stud was in his stomach. The waiters jumped in and grabbed Stipe's arms. He tried to break loose, still kicking in the magician's direction. "When you fucked the girl with the dick, then Stipe was okay! You faggot piece of shit, you…"

"See how he cooperates," Mungos said. He looked pleased.

"Hamlet's tactics," said Maskarin. "But you knew this before."

"Not everybody knew."

I wanted to know something else. "Is it true Stipe's the one who cuts the Americans now?"

"What Americans?" says Maskarin. "They just use that to screw around with him. With his whole family, for generations. And all this is his fault." He indicates Mungos with his head.

"He's the source of the story about the Americans."

"No way that's my fault," says Mungos. "Didn't I show you that American's funeral?"

"Fuck you! That was Dominik Ribarić, the diabetic. They cut off both his legs in America, so they buried him in the short coffin."

"You jerk!" says Mungos, now pretty upset. "Who'd bury people without legs in short coffins? It's all about dignity. They have the right to a long coffin. They invented the story when I figured out what was going on. As for whether Stipe's the one who cuts them or not, I don't know."

All this time of course I'm wondering if any of it's true. Striptiz had got pretty upset, so there might have been some truth in it, but on the other hand, screwing around with somebody like that was enough to make anyone lose control. Besides the strip business might be compromised because who was going to watch naked chicks at his place if they though he was sawing dead people in half. Who's doing the cutting today, or whether anybody is, that of course remains unknown, like a lot of things on this island, which can't even say exactly when noon falls.

7 THE BLACK SCHNAUZER

Making up's hard, and it takes a lot of alcohol. After the magic striptease fight, it took us a while to reconcile, while the tipsy lady from the box kept ice on her face, occasionally placing it in the glass of Bevanda in front of her. The belligerent parties sat at the same table until almost three in the morning. Mungos' make-up strategy, which consisted of frequent gestures to the waiter and nine bottles of Dingač, contributed a lot. But it didn't start that way.

Just after the fight two camps formed on the terrace. The first, which gathered around our table, consisted of locals: waiters, maids, and finally Stipe — two waiters still watching over him. Plump tourists on weight loss diets, mostly Czechs, a couple of journalists pretending to look for the animal, but who were in fact taking it easy because they were convinced it didn't exist, the magician's assistants, and the magician himself with the tipsy lady putting ice to his face gathered in the second camp, around the Tanzplatz and the broken cutting box. The two camps were at daggers drawn, and the main antagonists looked at each other with hostility.

Then there was a commotion in the opposite camp, the magician's. He struck the woman putting ice to his face, so now the assistants kept him from lunging at her, and she hissed some curse through her teeth. This caused an outburst of joy in our camp. Mungos even got up and went to pat the magician's shoulder. He said something in his ear and soon the whole hostile tribe moved to our table. The woman from the box was now putting ice to her face with theatrical flair, pretending to be insulted, and Mungos ordered a couple bottles of wine. This was how the hostilities concluded and a friendly hanging out began.

One of the journalists, who'd just returned from the front, talked about the shootings. He said during shootings in war the cross phenomenon always occurred.

"What's that?" I asked. I knew people were crucified but not that they were shot at the same time. The journalist said Jesus had carried his own cross and this was a part of his punishment, an act in which the executioner demonstrated full power over the one he was about to kill. People then got the impression the convict accepted his punishment. The same thing happened in war: those who were about to be shot often dug their own graves.

"Why do they do it?" I asked.

"Because they still hope!"

Now even the members of the warring tribes were listening to the story attentively, and a new solidarity had arisen among them. This was the story's purpose.

"Why do they hope?" the journalist went on. "They think it's not a real shooting. That's why false shootings exist. So the real ones can be carried out more easily."

By around three in the morning Stipe Striptiz had made up completely with his magic enemy, and while the magician was pulling marbles out of his ears, he publicly forgave him in front of everybody, like Christ forgave his murderers. He stood up, hiccupped twice, and informed us that he had to go home because his wife had to close the club. He was having trouble walking after all those bottles of Dingač, so I offered him my right shoulder. We joined forces and went together toward the fall tree and Stipe's ss joint…

At the door to his house, I delivered him to his wife and went into the club which, surprisingly, was still open. From all the alcohol, my body badly needed water. I found Franko, the receptionist from the Hotel Imperial, at the bar. In the old days, before the war, AIDS, Czechs, and health tourism, he used to tell us which rooms the solitary German and Italian girls were staying in, thereby reserving our lasting prayers for his final days. He used to say there were two kinds of women: cruel and boring. Cruel if they didn't put out, and boring if they did. The world's complexity lay in the fact that cruel women became boring with time and vice versa, which should fill every normal human being with existential horror, and that was just another term for chaos. His night shift obviously ended at half past four, and he was now at the bar gathering his strength before the meeting with his empty bed. In his youth he'd slept with more than three hundred women, mostly foreigners, but after his mother's death he'd been living completely alone, in a kind of widower's seclusion. He even neglected flirting, not so much for the fear of disease, but out of lost interest and a change of spiritual climate. Only now and then, people said, he'd sleep with some older lady, just to be able to buy dinner for his pals.

"I didn't see you at the funeral," I said. It was all I could think of.

"Ah, look at me," he said, "what would I do at a child's funeral? I neither made her nor fed her. I didn't even fuck her mother, that's a pity. Not that I wasn't at the funeral. But you know better…"

We were both quiet for a while, obviously thinking about our own pasts. I felt them intertwined here and there, like when we'd pulled off the brilliant Blitzkrieg on Škver with two Austrian girls who'd come to the island with some church group. I confess it was the fastest Blitzkrieg ever. Not even forty minutes had passed from intro to banging. A short school vacation. Franko's record was twenty minutes, they said, but the woman had long ago turned fifty, which cast a shadow over his great feat. I was sobering up, he was getting drunk for his encounter with the new day. So we sat at the bar in the strip club where tonight there was no stripping because the only female stripper, who actually wasn't a woman, had been murdered. I reached in silence for my glass of water untouched next to Franko's shot of Loza.

The day was dawning when we came out. There above Školijć and Dolin reddish tones mixed with the gray-blue of the morning light. We started toward town, but then we saw a little boy sitting on a stone curb next to the road, crying. He looked unreal in the morning landscape. I knelt down next to him. "Where's your mama?"

"She's working!"

Then Franko recognized him. "Tomislav, what are you doing here so early in the morning?"

Tomislav couldn't have been more than five. I noticed he had a tiny head.

"They stole my dog," he said.

"We'll look for him together," I said. I don't know why, I felt ready to promise anything.

But the kid burst into tears. Something inside him broke.

"Don't cry! We'll find him. He must have gone after some little bitch."

"No, he didn't run away," the kid sobbed. "He was stolen. The car hit him and then daddy buried him in the backyard. And then they took him."

"They took the dead dog's body?" This floored me.

"Take us to your house!" said Franko.

Tomislav was Striptiz Stipe's son. He brought us to the unfinished villa on Palit, right next to the SS club, where he lived with his parents. In the backyard, there was a little uncovered hole amid palm trees and agaves, like a grave for a newborn. It had obviously been dug in a hurry because dirt lay scattered all over the grass. There were no shoe prints or other visible traces.

They have a dog cemetery in Rijeka," said Franko. "They don't have to bury them in the gardens. They buy small plots of land and put up headstones."

"If we find him, we'll bury him in Rijeka, with a headstone and everything. Granny has a headstone, and I want Lord to have one too."

We stood over the open grave as we had three days earlier at Mirna's funeral. The same red dirt dotted with pebbles and dappled with roots sticking out of it, as from a severed arm.

"Stay home! Don't go out on the road, a car might hit you!" said Franko and rang the same door at which, not forty minutes before, I had delivered Stipe Striptiz like a mailman.

As we walked away I glanced back and saw the mother coming out of the house and putting a little blanket around the kid. He stood there over the empty dog grave in his yard and I could swear he was becoming smaller and smaller though we weren't moving away so fast.

"Maybe he was resurrected," I said.

"Who?"

"The Schnauzer. Maybe we're witnessing the birth of a new era, when dogs will get their own savior as well. *Ave regnum* Lord!"

"Stop bullshitting!" said Franko.

We separated at the school. Now it was broad daylight, and on my way home I couldn't stop wondering who would steal a dead dog's body and why. Things were stranger all the time.

8 TESTEN'S SIGN

The fourth noon, the one from the cathedral, must have woken me up because I didn't hear any other, and somewhere from behind a molar a rotten remnant of yesterday's sea bass swam forward like a nostalgic memory. I was just examining my bed linen when Mungos took me by complete surprise by appearing at my bedroom door.

"What the fuck are you doing?" he said as politely as he could.

"I'm checking to see if I vomited in bed."

There were no signs of it, which filled me with optimism. It was a great start to the day.

"What brings you here?" I asked. I didn't like the idea of policemen sneaking into other people's bedrooms, even if they were old friends.

"I'm going to see Marijan," he said. "I thought you might want to come along."

Driving in the Land Rover with police plates, we soon reached Kampor and the entrance to St. Euphemia's Monastery. Mungos stopped the car in a small parking lot above the entrance. Two other SUVs with plates I'd never seen before were parked there. From the sea down below, yelling and the clatter of a boat engine could be heard. Crickets buzzed in the tree tops, like a soft dentist's drill.

Mungos approached one of the Land Rovers, put his hand above his eyes to shield them from the bright light, and stared inside. Then we heard a voice from somewhere at the cemetery: "Fero, come here and I'll clean your ears!"

It was Marijan, who looked after Testen's heritage, and who used to take the wax out of my ears with a cotton-covered toothpick when I was a child. "So you can better hear the word of God," he'd say, though even then God's word had wandered through the waxed labyrinths of my auricle without reaching the right place. In the end, it still hasn't.

Friar Marijan came and kissed me, both hands holding my head, like a dear friend. For as long as I could remember, he'd always kissed me three times, on both cheeks and my forehead, Serbian Orthodox style. It was his contribution to ecumenism.

"Who are these intruders?" Mungos said, still staring into the dark interior of the vehicle.

Meanwhile, Marijan had lifted his cowl a bit and hurried, hopping in his Franciscan sandals on the gravel. He caught Mungos under the arm and quickly pulled him away from the incriminating Land Rovers.

He placed his index finger vertically over his lips, as if pointing to the tip of his nose instead of God. "Shhhhhh! I'll tell you everything. But let's have some cheese curds. After all, Fero's here."

It was evident right away Marijan felt uncomfortable about the cars and something strange was going on.

We passed through the church—a collection of Testen's oils showing the stages of the Cross hung on the left wall of the main nave—turned right, went through the monastery library, and reached a small gravel terrace overlooking St. Euphemia Bay. Soon after we were sitting at the wooden table in the shade of the vines, chewing excellent cheese curds from Lika, and sipping carob brandy.

"Do you know why this cheese squeaks?" said Mungos, cheese curds screeching in his mouth as he took a sip of brandy. "There was great poverty in Lika. Starvation. Children would get up at night and steal food. Then they'd eat it in their beds. So they came up with a cheese that made noise, so you couldn't chew it in secret, like in your bed at night."

"You invented that just now," I said, leaning over the rosemary and pressing its leaves to make them smell more.

"I did not! Ask anyone from Lika!"

What actually squeaks is our conversation. We talk about the screeching cheese so we won't have to talk about other, more important things. It's as if we're just warming up before the decisive matters. Squeak, squeak, squeak.

Meanwhile a large speed boat lands at the monastery's stone pier, and some friars gather their habits, under which I catch sight of jeans, and climb out of the boat. I notice it makes Marijan angry for some reason. He fidgets around the cheese and brandy, then moves them away from the table to a stone wall behind the rosemary. A secure location.

"Here are your intruders!" he says in answer to Mungos' question from ten minutes ago. "They eat and drink everything, like grasshoppers."

"And what are they doing here?" Mungos fires the main question, the one that probably brought us here in the first place. The cheese, of course, just happened by the by, as everything nice usually does.

"Eh, don't be such a snoop!" says Marijan, carefully following the movements of the people at the pier. They've loaded their bags and rucksacks on their backs and are climbing the path toward the monastery. "I told you I'll explain everything. Now wait for them to leave."

We grew quiet, the silence disturbed only occasionally by the dentist's drill in the cemetery pines and a quiet conversation in Italian that reached us slowly.

"Italians?" said Mungos.

"Shhhhh! Not all of them," Marijan said under his breath. "They understand!"

As they passed next to us, Friar Marijan's face stretched into an expression of incredible hospitality and meekness, and he mumbled "Jesus be praised" to the brothers, who nodded their heads one by one as they entered the shade of the monastery's atrium. All six of them. I couldn't miss the fact that one carried an open camcorder while a couple of them had cameras. Marijan watched as they passed, then returned the cheese and brandy to the table and said, "Today they're busy! Wait here,

I'll be right back!"

He disappeared in an instant somewhere inside the stone edifice. We waited for him in silence. Even the squeak of our chewing died out. The silence allowed me to remember Igor, who'd died just across the way, at Frkanj, at the sensitive age of seventeen, when dying's completely impractical. He'd run into a pine tree with his motorbike, and, they say, the pattern of the bark stayed on his forehead long after. His mother and sister fainted from crying, but they didn't know the embarrassing but tightly kept secret: afterward people all around the island said down there, in his underpants, he'd been wet. Probably he'd been playing with his heroic right hand up there above the nudist beach, and when they'd seen him, the nudes had run after him, so he'd had to hurry over all those bumps and roots to get away. But the magnificent Primorje pine had stood in the way of his clumsy wheels.

Later when I'd run into Igor's father at the cemetery, he'd always say Igor had been dead even before the pine cone had released its devil's seed there next to the forest path, before he'd even been born. He'd say all of us, when we used to go to Frkanj, had watched the killer grow, maybe even admired it, and he, his father, had more than once peed on its rough bark, which squeezed out tiny yellow resin tears. Maybe the tree had taken revenge on him for that. Eye for an eye, branch for a branch, son for a piss. That's how nature takes its revenge on us people.

Meanwhile Marijan came in discretely and entered my consciousness with care as if he were entering a funeral hall. Under his arm he carried a big portfolio with cardboard flaps, one of the ones Testen had used.

"You have to see this," he said, glancing around cautiously. "This is what those strangers of yours are studying now."

He opened the portfolio and leafed through the colorful drawings in ink. The motif was one and the same: a person looking at a lizard the size of a small crocodile in the monastery yard. The lizard was the same in each drawing, but the person watching it was different.

"What's this?" said Mungos impatiently, all policeman like.

"Look at this one," said Marijan, pointing at a man in front of the lizard. "It's Frane Španjol, the butcher. You can tell by his bloody apron. And this one," he said, lifting another drawing, "That's Bongo who used to smash glasses with his head in exchange for wine at the bar at Žurnal."

Mungos took one paper after another and carefully examined the characters. "Well, this one looks like Muki in his boat. He's got an oleander flower behind his ear."

"And look at this!" said Marijan, pulling out an intriguing drawing from somewhere below. It showed that same lizard, the same monastery yard, but in front of the lizard stood a naked woman with long red hair and distinct curves. The woman had a male sex organ between her legs and her testicles hung down prominently, as if weighted by gravity.

"It's the Match Girl!" yelled Mungos, astounded. "The gonorrhea woman!"

confess I was astounded too, and our two astonished faces stared at the strange drawing.

"Testen died eight years before she came to the island," he said again.

"Or he!" I clarified.

"That's the problem," said Marijan. "That's why the strangers are here. That's their interest. Besides, look, all these people standing in front of the lizard died strange deaths."

"What do you mean strange?" said Mungos, his chin dropping. "Didn't Frane Španjol die of a stroke? Natural causes."

68

"I don't mean strange for the police," Marijan explained.

"And what are the brothers doing here?"

"They're experts in *exorcizatio*."

"What?" asked Mungos.

"They're exorcists," I said.

9 LEICHENBEGLEITER'S LECTURE

War's an excellent time for holding a lecture on euthanasia on the island. The intellectual elite, I see, has gathered in the audience of the summer-time movie theater: Franka, the writer we once read for our book reports, Tomo, the lone fisherman intellectual, Egidio Franjina, the director of the psychiatric institution on Kampor, and a couple of old grannies who sit together in one row and gossip. The last probably came because they didn't know what euthanasia meant. Most likely it sounded vaguely catholic to them, like, for example, the Eucharist or Euphemia. Spending two hours of my afternoon in the sunny homeland here is a completely logical choice for a doctor for the dead. When Franka asked me to attend this medical lecture with its ethical implications, she explained it as physicians' solidarity with doctor Jungwirth, who obviously, besides delivering adverse diagnoses, was the local euthanasia activist.

As soon as I appeared at the entrance, Franka waved at me to sit next to her. She seemed to have long been saving a place for me in the front row, though there were plenty of others. In fact only two seats were taken. An older woman with ruptured capillaries on her cheeks and intense blue eyes, as if she'd used blue vitriol eye drops, sat beside her.

"This is Bepa," Franka said. "You remember Bepa, don't you?"

I recognized the woman who'd worked as a cleaning lady in our school twenty years before. She hadn't changed much. Her son had died in a car accident and at the time everybody had been full of understanding for her tragedy. But when the school toilet clogged up, it was she who still had to clean it. Shit all over the floor only two weeks after her son's death. He'd been burnt alive in a truck, while brownish pieces of shit floated in the yellow fluid all over the floor. We children watched her cry, her tears dropping into the disgusting water. The school principal, Mrs. Fruk, found her crying in the toilet. The lower hem of her blue duster was completely soaked in the stinky liquid. Mrs. Fruk began crying as well, and the two of them cried together over the dead son.

After that Bepa had been exempted from cleaning toilets. Her son's dead and she has to deal with shit. There's no dignity in that, they said. From then on she only did dignified things: making coffee, dusting books in the school library, Petrarch and Dante, with a moistened cloth, so as not to damage the paper of the immortal works.

During the following three years, as long as I attended the island school, Bepa grew calmer. She didn't forget her son, but she stopped mourning him so intensely. She forgot some of her misery, but she didn't go back to cleaning toilets. "Maybe when she gets a little tipsy, she's even grateful to her son for getting killed," Maskarin commented, seeing Bepa's occasional "happy" moods. "Maybe she says, 'Frane, thank you for getting me out of that shit. It wasn't for me. I was meant for something better, but fuck it; the child was born, I had to work to feed the family, and my husband, God rest his soul, was a drunk.'" "You're such a bastard," I'd told Maskarin. "A lawyer's about all you can become." We were eighth graders then.

"Bepa's retired now," Franka said. "She cleans books in the library part time."

I shook hands with Bepa.

"Is this Pipo's kid?" she said, although at forty I'm no kid anymore. It didn't surprise me she was holding up so well. I was certain she didn't plan on dying for a while. She'd had her portion of death a long time ago, just the right amount, so now it had to leave her alone for a while. She was entitled. She'd encounter it only at lectures like this one.

A wooden stand with a microphone was placed on the small stage beneath the screen, and next to it stood a table with sandwiches and snacks. So this is what attracted the old ladies, I thought. We waited in silence for the beginning of the lecture. Then a young man appeared from somewhere and began tapping the microphone membrane, saying one, one, one, like that Franciscan assistant at the funeral three days before. I was wondering whether this was the same mic when Leichenbegleiter climbed onto the stage, a paper in his hands. Maybe a euthanasia crib sheet.

Just as he began talking about the ethical aspects of euthanasia and European experiences in this field, one of the old ladies grabbed her chest and began frantically gasping for air, like a carp in a fish market. A woman from Primorje, breathing like a freshwater fish! Everybody jumped up, and the learned speaker left his crib sheet at the stand and came down to help. He was the only doctor around who treated live bodies. The director of the psychiatric institution and I just watched as he unbuttoned the old lady's shirt, took her pulse, and counted the tiny old heart beats with his stethoscope. Franka jumped in as well, I saw, and brought a glass of water for the old woman. But Leichenbegleiter was apparently satisfied with the heart beat, which didn't seem dangerous to him, so he returned to the stand.

"Momentary faintness," Franka repeated as she put the glass back on the table.

A second later those same European experiences from the Netherlands (the country most advanced in the treatment of human migration to the other world) are falling on us from the stage like bombs. The speaker talks about the free will of every rational human being to put his misery to an end, and another old lady, sitting next to the carp, suddenly yelps and grabs the lower part of her stomach as if, God forbid, her appendix has burst. Leichenbegleiter leaves his crib sheet again, but this time much more slowly. Franka hasn't jumped up so enthusiastically either. She's just rotated ninety degrees in her chair and now watches the doctor feel the lower part of the old lady's stomach over her black skirt. Meanwhile the director of the psychiatric institution just smiles.

"Now what?" Franka asks.

"The ladies were sent by the priest," says the director, "to sabotage the lecture."

All four old ladies got sick during the frequently interrupted lecture on departure by choice, and Leichenbegleiter intervened selflessly every time. To avoid being criticized for cruelty and out of fear that God might betray him by sending death for real to his lecture. But when it was all over, the old ladies hungrily dug into the sandwiches and mayo as if their lives hadn't been hanging from a thread just moments before. Then, marshaling her false teeth against the ham and stale bread, the old lady with whom I'd talked at Mirna's funeral approached me.

"Where's his fiancée?" the old lady asks, pointing at Leichenbegleiter.

"What fiancée?" I say, surprised I haven't yet heard the euthanasist has someone on the island. The granny must have mixed up something in her head, I think, and she says, "That little Romanian girl. The red one!!!"

The old lady explains to me that she saw them at Škver next to the heart clinic holding hands. She must have been the only one because nobody else on the island knew about it. Not even Mungos, who was getting good money to know a lot of things. The old woman wasn't aware she'd said something important. Or was it the priest's propaganda to blacken the doctor's name? With old ladies like that you never know where senility ends and wile begins. But then she said distinctly, "Where's that friend of yours from Zagreb?"

"What friend?" I hadn't brought any friends with me.

"The one from the funeral. Who talked about the doormat."

Things were honestly getting really bizarre. I'd been convinced that man was from the island. He knew everything about everybody and took me through the fauna of my own homeland so confidently. But I'd laid my eyes on him for the first time at the funeral.

"I don't know him," I say. "I thought he was from around here."

"The hell he is! I know everybody here, their children and grandchildren, from Zagreb, from Rijeka, wherever they're form. You're Pipo's boy, right?"

I had to admit she was right about that. My father was known as Pipo on the island. Because of his pipe.

But who the man at the funeral was—that was unclear. He'd seemed local to me.

Meanwhile Franka approached with the bald writer who read books on birds in her company. "Bobo made the sandwiches!" she said. Bobo was the writer. We'd never met officially. He offered his hand and was much nicer than at the library.

"Look at them chew!" he says, pointing at the old ladies as they torture themselves undeterred with the bread. "The priest sends them here to mine the lectures. And plus they get stuffed. That's why I serve sandwiches with stale bread. I arrange and decorate everything nice: olives, lettuce, mayonnaise, but the bread's so hard it makes you nuts. There's some pleasure in watching them suffer."

"Liar!" says Franka kindly. "You're not that mean. You're just too lazy to go to the store."

"Then I'm a liar," says the writer and winks as he walks over to the director of the psychiatric institution, who's talking to Bepa.

Franka takes my arm and drags me toward the exit. "His wife died three years ago. They spent their whole marriage, twenty years, living with the immobile old Miss who has no intention of dying just yet. No wonder he thinks about euthanasia. The old ladies get on his nerves."

We're walking down the shiny stone tiles of the narrow street toward Piazzetta. The afternoon has grown late and is slowly turning to evening. The sun leans above Frkanj Peninsula, painting the bay pink. We walk in silence. She holds onto me like an old friend, and I'm afraid of touching her naked skin. We watch the sun.

"Have you noticed the days are getting so much shorter?" she says.

"Yes," I reply, and wait for her to say something else. But the silence lasts, the silence of a man and a woman who've known each other half their lives but between whom nothing ever managed to happen. I finally ask, "What do you do with the books with the ripped out endings?"

"Throw them away. What else would I do with them?"

"Maybe Bepa's doing it? So she has less to clean."

"I don't believe that," she says. "But anything's possible."

At moments like this everything does seem possible. We had dinner after.

10 SAHARA

The full moon kept the fishermen in their houses and lured the wackos and tourists out onto the street. When we came out of the restaurant, we heard the wild voices of the night bathers from the town's beach. Later we saw a group of skinny dippers running toward the Roman cemetery. Their naked behinds gleamed white among the ancient stones.

"How long has it been since you saw Sahara?" says Franka.

"Since I was young," I say. "Why?"

"We could have a swim."

I thought things were moving in some unknown and dangerous direction but didn't say anything.

Soon we were speeding in her light blue Beetle toward the most exotic beach on the island, a perfect desert—the Sahara—made of grayish sand that offered a view of the contours of Goli Otok and Sveti Grgur. In my youth I'd often bring women I wanted to have sex with here. Mostly Germans. This thing with Franka was something exotic. All the time we were driving toward Lopar, the moon was right in front of us, turning the darkness of the Mediterranean into a polar night, like something from a Bergman film. I observed Franka keeping her eyes on the road and thought about her profile. It seemed to me it had changed a little, something with the forehead and nose proportions, I couldn't say exactly. The rare cars coming from the opposite direction would light her whole face for a moment with bright reddish or yellow light, like in a sunset, then everything would sink back into a dim bluish haze.

All of a sudden her face became contorted and with an expression of horror turned toward me to look at something on my side. By the roadside I saw a little blonde girl standing in the moonlight completely alone, as if hypnotized. I thought of Mirna, the girl we'd said goodbye to three days before. Anyhow it looked a lot like her. Franka continued driving as if nothing had happened, her face back to normal.

More than a minute passed before I said, "Go back! We have to see what that was!"

"So you saw it too," she said, with what sounded like relief in her voice. She put the car in reverse and we carefully went back those couple hundred feet to where we'd seen the girl.

Stories about the sudden appearances of dead people are part of island lore. There used to be a butcher shop called Frane's in Srednja Street. It stood there for ages. The owner and the only employee was Frane Španjol. Up until '65. Then across the way from Frane's meat boutique a big bull's head with the sign BUTCHER in red letters between its horns suddenly appeared. Some company from Rijeka had opened it. Frane got so upset that one morning he had a stroke. When they carried him out of the shop, still wearing his bloody apron, he was dead.

"He's going to the fridge, following his dead legions," the shell souvenirs' seller quipped, leaning against the door frame of his shop. That's when the trouble started. Frane's wife employed a qualified butcher from Cres and the shop continued its work. But the one across the street worked too. The customers were divided between those faithful to tradition and those open to novelty. The new butcher shop had special lights, all the meat was pink, and the selection was better too. The restaurant owners, traditionally the most flexible, slowly turned toward progress and better lit meat. But not for long. The news spread that they'd sold stinky tenderloins to the owner of the Alibaba Inn, which caused a scandal on the island. The manager of the new butcher shop swore the meat was fresh, but in vain. People started talking, whispering in the street, many had experiences with stinky meet. But at the same time they knew the man, the supplier. He supplied both the new and Frane's shop with the same meat. But at the bull's head it stank.

"This can't be right," commented the old women at the market. "Something's wrong about this."

News spread around the island it was dead Frane stinking up his competitor's chops. Work of the devil. How could the supplier be the same and one meat stinks while the other doesn't? So people began avoiding the bull's head. Housewives stopped looking into the shop window because they didn't want to meet the manager's eyes, and the meat waited for customers and stank. Later somebody carved FRANE into the bull's head with something sharp.

But what we'd seen by the road wasn't fiction, it was a real little blonde girl. When Franka stopped the car where we'd seen her, nobody was there. Even stranger was the fact that there were no houses. It was hard to imagine someone letting a child wander alone by the road at that time of night.

"I don't like it that we're seeing things," she said, as I got out of the car. I walked to the spot where I thought the child had stood. There was nothing, only some Maquis brush lit by the moonlight, quivering in the gentle breeze. I looked farther down the road, then around the nearby hill. Nothing. Suddenly I heard the sound of a rolling pebble. As if somebody had hastily stepped on it. I listened carefully, uncomfortable but moving forward anyhow into the brush. Meanwhile Franka sat in the safety of the car. Twenty meters more and still nothing. To comfort myself, I unzipped my fly and began to pee, urinating on my fear, as it were.

Back at the car I saw Franka leaning against the wheel, staring dully in front of her, the knuckle of her index finger in her mouth.

"There's nothing here," I said. I left out the pebble.

We moved on. Franka put a tape into the cassette player, and soon Bob Zimmerman began singing "Knock, knock, knockin' on the heaven's door" in his frog's voice. A song from our youth. It improved our mood somewhat. We were just passing the Zlatni Zalaz restaurant, where once long ago my life had reached its prime — bottle of Postup, two pounds of stewed shrimp, metallic gold BMW with racing suspension, and Konstanza Brunner, a red haired German from Braubach, owner of BMW. That night God had been my best friend.

"What are you thinking about?" Franka asked.

"Pussy," I said. "You?"

"Me too," she said. "My own."

We grew silent. Anything else we might have said would have made things too sad. Dylan now sang a gentle song about Sara, his ex-wife, who, when they got divorced, took six million dollars from him.

"Have you ever drunk wine under water?"

Franka seemed to have completely forgotten about the girl. Her face looked happier.

"Look under the seat," she said. "Must be a bottle of Plavac there."

"I see you're well equipped," I said. Though she was a virgin, I had to admit she didn't miss out on all the valuable experiences. About the wine I said I'd never drunk anything under water except water, but that had been a long time ago, when I was learning to swim.

When the Lopar road brought us to the turn off for Sahara, Franka stopped the car. We sat for a while without saying anything.

"I don't think I'm in the mood for walking down to Sahara," she said.

The little girl by the road must have shaken her.

"Then let's go to the camp," I said. It had one of the most beautiful beaches on the island.

Luckily the beach guard wasn't there so we could drive onto the wet sand, leaving meandering tracks behind us. As soon as we stopped, Franka began taking her clothes off. Her naked body in the confined space of the car made me uncomfortable, so I applied myself to opening the bottle. When we got out, everything got easier. I saw her skinny figure, the horrible asymmetry of her breasts, her red nipples, like bonbons for children, and the black triangle of her pubic hair. It seemed on the whole more geometrical than human, which offered a sort of relief. She immediately ran shouting through the water, and the moonlight momentarily turned the droplets into little stars.

I ran after her carrying the bottle. Here the water was shallow, so we had to go rather far from shore to be able to submerge properly. Franka did it first. She encircled the neck of the bottle with her lips, as if it was a dick, and vanished underwater. I assumed she was drinking but didn't know what she was doing with her nose. She stayed under for quite a while, so long I almost got worried. When she came out, at least two deciliters of the wine were gone.

"You're really good," I said, taking the bottle, and went down. I too had to take the neck of the bottle fully into my mouth like a male sex organ, which was something completely new for me. I used my other hand to hold my nose and plunged into the underwater adventure. It must have been like this in the uterus, I thought, tasting the bitter fluid that mixed with salty water in my mouth.

"I did it!" I yelled after I'd sprung out of the water, choking on the blood of God, a small portion of which had gone down the wrong way. I felt as though I'd just been born—I swallowed deep breaths of air that would allow me to cry for the first time.

But Franka didn't notice me. She stood up to her breasts in the water with her back to me, staring at something on shore.

"What's wrong? Somebody stealing our clothes?" I asked, feeling good. The Plavac must have had something to do with that.

"Look!" she managed to hiss. The sound of her voice made me freeze.

There on the shore I could make out the figure of the little girl we'd seen by the road. She stood completely still, lit by the moonlight, looking at us.

11 HOPSCOTCH

Morning. After a sleepless night, Franka and I walk arm in arm down the boardwalk, looking inside the yachts. A life we never had. Mementos of missed opportunities. Franka says, "I always felt nauseous on boats."

I suppose that's a curse for somebody born on an island. But actually there aren't that many yachts. Only a few regular guests not even war can stop from observing the destiny of this country from the inside of their vessels.

I finally say aloud what has been on my mind all the time, "Why did you think that was Mirna?"

"Because I think I've been seeing dead people lately. But you don't understand."

In front of the post office we see a man tear a piece of paper into tiny bits, scatter them all over the ground, and then bend down to pick them up.

"After Nativity they start letting them out," she says.

I still remember the ladies in strange hats and grannies in bathroom robes with flowery motifs, who bummed cigarettes. They'd begin appearing on the boardwalk and on Srednja Street some time in mid September. Locked up during the main season, in early autumn the inhabitants of the psychiatric asylum would mingle among the Austrian retirees and high school excursion groups, coloring the fall.

I tried to cheer her up by telling her that for Christmas the year before I'd decided to buy an artificial penis for my ex-wife. But as I entered the porn store in Gajeva Street in Zagreb, I noticed the salesman was a dwarf. In general I feel respect for dwarfs because they make the space around them seem surreal, but this dwarf insulted me. He showed me the vibrators, tested their speed, and demonstrated how they worked. But I felt more and more repulsed. Some of the artificial members, especially the black ones, were almost a fifth of the dwarf's full height, which gave the grin on his face an especially ironic twist. He saw me out of the store with that grin on his face, and I felt it on my back like a summer sunburn, not painful, but prickly.

And so, analyzing dwarfs and dildos, we reached the Hotel Istria and the entrance to the park. Two police vehicles were there, definitely too many for the usual patrol. Only then did we notice little groups of locals from nearby stores and the tourist office discussing something in low voices. For a moment the atmosphere reminded me of after the funeral: a kind of conspiratorial solidarity. Next to one of the kiosks with the usual wooden knickknacks, carved donkeys and lacquered egrets stood Tomo, gesticulating and explaining something quietly to the people around him. The expressions on their faces told us that something serious had happened.

"Has somebody died?" asked Franka. It was the first thing that came to her mind of course, considering the way things had been going.

"No, no one died," said Tomo absentmindedly, "it's even worse."

He hurried up the stairs toward the terrace of the Imperial. Without a word he loped up the hill, and Franka and I followed like a Partisan column. As we climbed, Franka whispered how she'd been in love with Tomo long ago, in elementary school, when he'd been most active with the German women. Then she noticed my sour expression and said, "I loved you too. Just differently."

From the terrace Tomo continued up the hill toward the cemetery. He hadn't turned back once. He seemed to have forgotten us and was completely consumed by the thought leading him on.

"He's going to the cemetery!" she said. "I'm not going any further."

I grabbed her arm firmly. "I'll protect you," I said, as if that meant anything.

So the two of us, like the accused and the bailiff, hopped toward the iron gates. In front two policemen were smoking. One said, "Fero, Mungos was asking about you…"

Things were more bizarre by the minute.

Tomo, who'd also passed by the guards on account of his

connections, was rushing in big strides down the main alley to the west, the new part of the cemetery. In one of the side paths, where we turned following Tomo's bent back, a hopscotch was drawn on the asphalt, laid out like a double cross. It was something I'd never expected to see in a cemetery. A piece of brick lay in one of the squares, as if someone had stopped the game in a hurry.

A second later in front of us a yellow line with POLICE written on it appeared. It was like some sort of a ramp. More uniformed policemen were standing there, hats off, sweaty shirts wide open. Mungos was above the open grave with a camera, and an older policeman was taking a plaster cast of a footprint from the ground. Tomo, being a civilian, stayed on the other side of the yellow line and stared into the open grave, nervously picking up remnants of the piled up wreaths. The inhabitant of the small white coffin was no longer there, only a disgusting, sweet, smell I knew well wafted up of the grave.

"An exhumation?" I asked, astonished.

"Not an exhumation, no," Tomo said. "They stole the body last night!"

Just as two days before at the funeral, the light of a camera flash blinded us. Franka stood next to me in silent disbelief, covering her nose and mouth with her hand. Meanwhile, a policeman who'd climbed into the grave said something from inside that sounded like, "So little, still stinks so bad!"

Mungos came up, took another shot from our civilian perspective, and put his hand on my shoulder. "Fero, tell me, as a pathologist, where would you hide a little girl's body if you wanted to preserve it?"

My mind was drawn to the hopscotch, though I hoped the vicinity of the open grave and the hopscotch on the ground was accidental. It was hard to imagine that, at night or on a morning like today's, little girls, some more than a hundred years old, would leave their graves to play. Hop, skip, one, two, three.

"Have you seen the hopscotch?" I asked Mungos.

"It's got nothing to do with this," Franka said. "Some child got bored. I was bored too at the cemetery when I was little."

"I'm not so sure it has nothing to do with this," I said. "From here it looks like a cross turned upside down."

"What does it mean?" asked Mungos.

"It's satanism!"

The Island of Shadows

I GRAY CITIZENS

A child's funeral is like a princess farting on a pea: the stench suddenly stinks up the fairytale. But it stinks even worse when two days later the child vanishes from the grave, and a thick fog falls upon the town. Like in books by that writer who gives hard bread to the old ladies. Slowly, like a blind man in front of a great expanse of white, I descend the narrow alley toward Srednja Street. A thin damp film has settled on the worn out street tiles. I slide more than walk in my leather-soled summer moccasins, unsuited to the wet island autumn. The lives of those whose feet wore down these tiles are wrapped up in their slipperiness. This is never more obvious than on foggy days like this. As if our beloved dead were tripping us up to make us hit the stones dug with such pain at Goli Otok. The war up there on the Velebit, too, is being fought more or less because of the dead. Such are my thoughts this foggy morning two days after the disappearance of Mirna's body, as I tap my way down the right side of an empty alley, hugging the wall and metal rail. Then I see somebody coming from the opposite direction. Or is he just standing in the street close to St. Anthony's Church? The dark silhouette of a lonely passer-by. But something's wrong with the silhouette. Its posture is strangely stiff.

It reminds me of Franka's unnatural rigidity from some twenty years back when I once pressed my lips against her earlobe. Someone was drilling holes for the metal part of an awning. She was in front of me and I could see little flaky white hairs on her neck shining with sweat. The sound of the drill was very loud, and it crossed my mind that in that noise, when words can take on all kinds of meanings, I should say I love her just like that. Maybe she'd stop and ask me what, and I'd tell her I hadn't said anything and she'd turn toward the terrace of the Hotel Grand and I'd say it again. The worst thing was I wouldn't have known why I did it. Anyway I didn't say anything and we walked down onto Srednja Street in front of the pharmacy. And it's all just like now, walking down before the stranger whose posture's so odd and stiff. I almost walk right into him in the fog. And then what a shock!

The silhouette isn't a person's at all though the shape is human. It's as tall as an average man. It stands next to the nearby filigree store as if calling up memories of crocheted silver brooches from the empty window. For I see the store's closed and the goods safely stored until the next tourist season. I walk round the silhouette, which is made of thick gray sheet metal with a heavy cast iron base. It has the contours of a person and is dangerously similar to the man-shaped targets at shooting ranges. Only without the holes. What's this thing doing here? It was obviously put here at night or early in the morning because I didn't see it last night on my way home. To make matters more complicated, there's no one in the street to ask. A moment of thought, will I go left and down the boardwalk, or right down Srednja? The destination's the same, Café Sutjeska, where the islanders meet when all the hotel terraces and cafes close for the season.

But on the plateau in front of the café another gray shape juts out from the fog. Hurrying past, I almost say hi. Because now, after the season's over, all the islanders greet each other like hikers. This one looks even more like a man, though with somehow misshapen facial features in the fog. I'm thinking about it as I enter Sutjeska. Tomo, Muki and Maskarin are sitting in the booth on the right, and one of those animal journalists, who must have just returned from the front because he's all muddy, is explaining to them how at night our commandos stab their soldiers in the necks with knives. He's rolled the newspaper into a long tube, a faux bayonet, and he smacks a spot on Muki's neck with it.

"What the fuck is this?" I say, sitting down next to the bewildered Muki, who seems as if he's just been slain.

"What?" asks Tomo.

"Those steel sheets."

"Gray citizens," says Maskarin. "There's one by the pharmacy, and I've seen one behind the school. On the way down to the marina."

"No one knows what it means or who they are," Tomo adds. "My cousin says they're our people who've been killed in the war, and the council put the monuments up before the announcement. There was a big offensive last week. They'll carve in the names later."

"That can't be it," says the journalist. "Because you know everything right away. I mean, you see it on TV. Who lost his leg, who's dead, who ran away. You can't hide it just like that. I think it's something else."

Then he lowers his head and signals with his hand to come nearer, it seems, for something confidential. He says: "They put them close to the Serb houses so they know what's going to happen if they don't leave. The one near the marina is right below the council member Slavko Tadić's house. But it's not good to talk about it. The foreign press will find out, and then they'll just fuck us up the ass in their media."

"What about the one here, in front of Sutjeska?" I say. "As far as I know, there aren't any Serbs here."

His whole theory seems shaky.

"The council is here," says the media rep, as if he's explained everything by that, and then goes on, "There's a rumor around the island the Serbs dug up little Mirna and people have had enough."

"Really!" Muki blurts out, shocked as if his kindness has been threatened. The rest of us, a little smarter by tradition, look at the media rep suspiciously. But he's persistent: "I've heard the doctor, the kid's mother, had somebody around and he knocked her up. But when he knocked her up she married Globus 'cause the other one was married. And the married guy was a Serb. Before he left, he dug up his daughter from her grave. I heard they do these things up there in Lika, take their dead with them. And listen, other Serbs from the island helped him. That's why now they want them to go away. It's not fair, them plowing up our soil to take their dead out. They've been here ever since the Cominform. They're all former guards from Goli."

But Mungos says, "You're so full of bullshit!"

And the conversation is suddenly over. Mungos gets up from the table, pays what there is to pay at the bar, and all four of us say goodbye to the journalist, who, somewhat taken aback, watches our maneuver.

"I haven't insulted you, have I?"

"No, you haven't," says Mungos. "You're just full of bullshit!"

Outside the fog hasn't yet lifted though it's eleven already. We walk across the boardwalk toward the police station because Mungos has to meet the police team from Rijeka.

"That guy's full of shit," Mungos says. "You never know

who people like him work for, they just fuck around with us with their stories."

"Renata wouldn't pass off somebody else's child," says Tomo.

"You never know," I say.

When we reached the police station, a dark blue BMW with one red and one blue light on its roof stood in the reserved lot. It looked like a man with different colored eyes, only very official. Behind it there was a police wagon with forensic tools in aluminum suitcases in the trunk and on the back seat.

"They're here!" says Muki, gulping and looking worried.

Why would Muki be worried about forensics?

2 DEBT COLLECTORS

The afternoon brought a north-easterly we call the Bura, and the Bura sent the fog away. Patches of transparent sky opened above the town, and the gray citizens grew long afternoon shadows. Only now, after the grayish curtain had lifted, could we see how many there were. People crawled out onto the boardwalk. It was all they talked about. They gathered around the flat statues in little groups like natives around aliens, touched them with their hands, knocked against their metal surfaces, some even tried to lift them. The fact that they weren't fixed to the ground, I don't know why, caused relief. In the company of a metal citizen, standing all the way at the end of Vela Riva, at the breakwater next to the light house, I found Leichenbegleiter.

"This is unbelievable," said the corpse chaperon slash euthanasia activist. "They're so many, but nobody knows anything."

I told him it actually wasn't that unbelievable for an island where many things were unknown by tradition.

"Yes, yes," he said, "but something as big as this can't happen without the Council and island authorities. Someone brought all this here by boat and set it up. What's unbelievable is nothing leaked out."

An old man next to us, a boat farer wearing an old over tight shirt with grease and salsa spots on it said, "There's one on Frkanje, on the way to the nudist beach!"

"I heard a company from Rijeka put them up. I think they're black statues for collecting debts."

My and Leichenbegleiter's mouths dropped open in surprise.

"This happens out in the world," said the old man. "In London. When somebody owes money, a gentleman in black stands in front of his store: derby hat, umbrella, and a tailcoat. He doesn't beat him, he doesn't curse his donkey mother, he just stands there like that day after day. And the customers avoid the debtor. There the greatest shame is being in debt."

"Then why are there no people standing here, just metal sheets?" asked Leichenbegleiter, showing some genuine interest in the story.

"That's us," the old man said. "You can't pay someone to stand in front of the store here. Especially if you count standing as work. Our people can only stand and do nothing if it's not work. Besides, it's too much money to pay their salaries, taxes, retirement, you name it. That's why they came up with these metal people, but they forgot they can be moved. Somebody moved this one here, to the Riva, so we wouldn't see who it is owes money in town."

Leichenbegleiter and I, brimming with this new knowledge, went along the boardwalk toward town. It didn't seem convincing that debts would be collected that way here. It was also somehow too pacifist for this latitude. Besides, the statue on Frkanj didn't fit because there were no houses, businesses, or restaurants. I'm thinking all this over as we approach town and the Council building. The corpse chaperon walks calmly by my side immersed in his own thoughts. It crosses my mind that maybe, unconsciously, he's following me. But where to? I watch his steps, trying to make out where he's going, if he's got a route at all. When I see him tending straight toward Hotel Istria, I veer off quickly with a light hand shake. A man, if he's all there, should set himself apart from the corpse chaperon as soon as possible, before passing neighbors start feeling sorry for him. Anyhow, there are too many dead people on the island as it is. I turn toward St. Christopher's Square with the intention of stopping by to see Franka at the library.

I meet her talking to one of the painters on the stairs. In front of him are paintings of Marilyn Monroe and Einstein in stylized black and white crayon. Both have white hair and look somewhat alike. Einstein's sexy and Marilyn's intelligent. Franka looks intelligent too while she discusses the portraits' problems with the amateur master. The master, I see, is hitting on her, but Franka, as usual, doesn't notice. I come up from behind, like an old beast, and lay my hand on her shoulder. Just to make the master angry. I keep it there for a second and give her a gentle squeeze, as if to say, here I am, friend.

"You won't believe this," I say. "But the corpse chaperon followed me here!"

"The who???" says Franka in genuine disbelief.

"Leichenbegleiter!"

Who's that?" she asks as if she's just heard the word for the first time. Now I'm the one in disbelief. What kind of collective amnesia rules over this island?

I repeat the story I heard from the would-be friend at the funeral: "Jungwirth. He worked as a doctor in Rijeka, his patients often died. His colleagues started sending him their patients, the terminally ill ones, so he could break the news. So they called him Leichenbegleiter, corpse chaperon. He bought a woven doormat, a regular jute mat, and put it inside his office door…"

I break off. Franka's looking at me as if I'm one of the living dead she's been seeing.

"It's the first time I've heard this story," she says and turns back to the master to say goodbye. Then she takes me under the arm quickly, as if returning that friendly pat from a second before, and we start off down Srednja Street toward the pharmacy. The tourists are gone. The foggy day has chased them all away. Only a few European retirees or yacht owners with time on their hands stroll down the empty street, peeking into the closed stores.

"You know, I've known Jungwirth for years. It's completely normal that his patients died because he's an oncologist. Everything else is crazy. I've never heard about this nickname, and I don't know why you're spreading such stories around."

I see I've unintentionally insulted her.

"I'm sorry," I say, but actually I think patients, even friend-patients, never know the subtle nicknames of their doctors. That's actually normal, otherwise they wouldn't be their patients. Or their friends for that matter. I move on to something else.

"When's the fiesta?" I ask.

"Day after tomorrow," Franka says. "I hear they're preparing something special. It has something to do with these statues."

"Some old guy says that's how debts are being collected around here."

"They look more like targets to me. That's in fashion these days."

The store keepers stand at the entrances of the rare filigree stores still open and call to each other. Every few steps Franka greets somebody and I think life in a small town, if you're polite, is reduced to constant nodding. Your neck hurts from politeness. They respond with a dose of pity, at least that's how it seems to me. As if the dying are going past.

"The forensics squad from Zagreb is here," I say after a brief silence.

But Franka doesn't seem ready to talk about the dead. Especially not about the stolen dead. So she's silent after my remark.

"Let's have a latte at the Istria," she says, a latte seeming the cure for the dead's encroachment on our ever more unpleasant lives. It's an advance that, on this island, borders on impoliteness. So we turn toward the Istria and its pleasant little café, where the view opens onto the entrance into town and a good portion of the boardwalk.

We've stopped at the bar and just begun forgetting. We've taken a short intermezzo between all the necrophilia, when Frenki Španjol, who runs the ski school, turns up suddenly in front of us. They've called him Skišul for years because of the "Ski Schule" sign on his speedboat. People around town say he loves really young girls, even too young to be legal. All handsome, blonde, and tanned, he supposedly sleeps with most of his students from the Ski Schule and sometimes with their mothers too. Of course, never at the same time. He takes turns, a true Catholic. His view is that even in sin you have to be modest. He comes up to us from one side and hugs Franka like an old friend. It's her biggest problem: all men hug her like friends.

"You've heard what people are saying, right?" says Skišul, visibly disgusted, without a hello. "They found an upside down cross next to the kid's little grave. Satanists must have taken her out."

Maybe it's logical that Skišul as a declared pedophile is the one most disgusted by the child's death. He probably feels the loss most acutely.

"We were up there," says Franka. "But I didn't see any crosses."

She seems to have forgotten the hopscotch on purpose.

"You remember last winter when our graves got spoiled? Somebody relieved himself on my late uncle's grave. I'd taken my old lady to visit her brother, I think it was Sunday. I'm pushing her wheelchair through the park toward the grave, and then, right in the middle of it, a huge piece of shit. Somebody even wiped himself with newspaper. I'm looking at the headlines, the newspaper's from before the war, a story on the Rijeka-Velež soccer match. I pick up the newspaper and am reading. I wasn't scared my old lady might faint because she was sitting in the wheelchair. Let her faint all she wants. But instead of fainting, she says, 'Frano, remove that shit so we can pay our respects!' Satanists did that."

"Those weren't Satanists," says the bartender, who comes from Pag every season to work. "In his time, that cousin of his had sent half the island to the prison on Goli Otok. That's why they shit on his grave. It's tradition, not Satanism."

"Other graves were desecrated too," says Skišul, offended because the seasonal worker from Pag has interfered with his diagnosis. "The crosses were pulled out and turned upside down."

"Kids," says the worker challengingly.

"As if kids can't be Satanists. I know what they do. I was

a kid on this island. And so was Fero. Had they given us ten years on Goli, it wouldn't be enough for all we did. Isn't that right, Fero?"

He winks in my direction as he says this, reminding me of all the stupid things we did together. I'm still trying to forget all that, even today.

3 FRIAR MARIJAN

Getting a job as a policeman is one way of answering the ever-lasting philosophical question of why we die. The clergy provides the answer to the question's second part, where we go after we die. And medicine tries to answer the third part, why we stink when we're dead. Then they mutually inspire each other quite nicely. That's why I wasn't surprised when Friar Marijan and Mungos appeared together at the entrance to the Istria's café. Both wore civilian clothes, but in their eyes you could catch a glimpse of their uniforms, each his own. Things were obviously getting complicated.

Mungos says "Fero" even before they've sat down next to us at the bar. "You still haven't told me where you'd hide the kid. True, it's getting chillier, but it's not so chilly that the stench wouldn't get around."

But the bartender, as if he's being paid for his comments instead of for pouring drinks, jumps in again. "Excuse me, but on Pag we know all about that."

"All about what?" says Mungos, curiosity in his voice, as if he senses something of interest.

"About the dead. Let me tell you about what happened when I was ten. I was fishing with my father here in the channel, and the Bura threw us up toward Lun. We were about to hit the rocks there behind Pižnjak. The sea was boiling over, getting completely out of control. My father was worried, I could tell, that we were going down. Then he somehow threw the anchor and slowly, dragging on the rope, we reached some cove, pulled the boat half way out, and tied it to some rocks on two sides. In a vise. Couldn't move even if it wanted. We get ashore, take our stuff out, the wind hitting us all the time. I'm completely frozen. No fat on me whatsoever. The wind could go through my ribs."

"What has this got to do with the kid?" say Skišul, a little suspicious.

"You'll see. When we get our stuff out, my father finds this cave and we hide there from the wind. I was so fucking scared because people were saying there were ghosts on that side of Lun. A couple of fishing boats had capsized there. My old man tells me to find some wood to make a fire or we're going to freeze. The sun's already down and it gets dark, and the Bura's getting stronger and stronger. And when you're scared, wind is the worst thing. You hear strange sounds. So I look for the wood, but I can't see any. Only some dried up weeds, no wood anywhere. I'd gone pretty far from my father, it was completely dark, then I saw some kind of a pile. It looked like wood. I ran up and saw some worm eaten boat planks. I thought somebody had gotten killed here. It was ready to make a fire. I start collecting the planks, praying to God and Jesus. I mean, what could I do? The Bura's blowing hard, it's already dark, everything looks horrible all around. When I've got as much as I can carry, I turn my back to the wind. And then!!! Shadows. Some twenty meters in front of me. Like those outside there. I thought they were people so I went closer to see. But when I saw them, I almost died. Dead people! Four of them! Their hair flying in the wind. They looked like they were dancing."

"How'd you know they were dead?" says Mungos, winking at us. "Was there a sign on their skulls?"

"Fuck, no sign, no, but I could see. They're completely naked, with just some rugs around their asses. Totally dried up like skeletons. But then again they weren't skeletons. They had faces and hair, and the dried up skin wrinkled up around their bones. I started running, threw the wood away, fell down two or three times on the sharp rocks, it didn't hurt at all. I reached my father and told him the dead people were coming after us. I'd seen them. Father had just taken out some sausage to eat something, and when he heard me, he grabbed me by the arm and we went back. I almost shat my pants. I told him, 'Dad, there are dead people!' He didn't say a thing. He just dragged me by the hand. When we got there, we stopped right in front of them. Not even ten meters away. I'm telling myself, 'This is a bad dream. It can't be real!' But they just stood there."

"Did you at least piss your pants?" asks Skišul. "I'd pee and shit myself both, all at once."

"Shut up, don't interrupt. I didn't shit or pee on myself. Only my nose was running. I couldn't stop the snot. It was the only time that ever happened to me, never since. I almost choked on my own snot. Then my father says, 'This one here, with the gray hair, that's Antun Kunkera, and the one next to him is Friar Radovan.' I look at my father, he seems to be talking to them. He isn't scared. Only then do I see they're tied against some posts."

Here the island *Gastarbaiter* paused for a moment and took a sip of Pelinkovac he kept under the counter. To lube himself a little.

"So what happened?" asked Franka impatiently. Obviously, she was the only one who believed him.

"Our friars dry the dead people on this side of Lun. My father told me about it then. They have an ossuary in the monastery's basement, where they prepare the well-known people from the island. Then they stack them. Later we saw more of them. You could recognize faces on some of them. There were even children."

"They dry dead people???" Franka asked, as if she'd come down to this archipelago from the moon. There just wasn't anything like this in her world. Probably why she'd stayed a virgin.

"I've heard all kinds of things, but this..." says Skišul. "I heard we cut them, but you drying them, now that's something."

"Impossible," I say. "Most of the year is so warm here that the body would spoil. Maybe up in Norway, where the wind blows all the time, but not here. You'd need wind every day and a lot lower average temperature."

"But if you brine them? The Bura's salty here, right?"

"Not even if you brine them," I say with confidence, expert on the dead that I am.

"So it's just a story," says Franka, relieved. "Same as ours about somebody cutting them up."

"Besides, the vultures would eat them," I explain. Posthumous bio-hygiene.

All this time Friar Marijan is silent. A strange expression of disgust covers his face and seems to say, "Just listen to yourselves! Listen, you sinners!" He himself doesn't say anything. He's just disgusted, which isn't usual for him, and he sips the espresso the eloquent bartender has placed in front of him. Maybe he knows something about how to dry the dead but doesn't want to talk about it. Friars on these islands know all kinds of recipes.

Then suddenly the expression on his face intensifies, and God's servant makes for the restroom as if he wants to shit all over this discussion and more. While the consecrated character is emptying his bowels in relief behind the closed door with HERREN written on it, Skišul has already started in on a story about him. "Fero, did you know Marijan's not his name? They're just screwing around with him."

"No, I didn't."For as long as I can remember he's been Marijan. I don't know him by any other name.

"What's this all about now?" says Franka, accusation in her voice. She obviously doesn't like this story about Marijan.

"Where have you ever seen a friar called Marijan? His church name is Jerolim, nobody knows his civilian name."

"If you're going to bullshit, say it right now," says Franka. "So we can leave. I don't have to listen to this crap."

"Let the man talk," says Mungos in his police voice, with a security glance toward the restroom door.

"That was back in the sixties. He was a young friar, he came to the island to bless the island people as if he'd come to Africa. A fucking missionary. And those from the council hated him more than anything."

"Your cousin too, right?" says the bartender from Pag.

"Will you leave him alone?" says Mungos nervously, afraid the story will slip away like an oil-covered eel. Because friar Marijan, whose isn't actually Marijan, might be done shitting any second and interrupt the story just as it was getting most interesting. So the expert goes on with the story from his childhood, from when he'd have probably got a hard on from his own ass even. "And so he met up with some Slovenes at that vacation home that belonged to the Štore Hardware

Company, up there on Marijan Hill. They get drunk. The friar has a couple too. It's no sin among the pious… And they sing Slovenian and Croatian national songs. So they get to the one "Marjane, Marjane!!!" with the verse: "A na drugoj strani Zrinski Frankopani (And on the other side the Zrinski Frankopans)."

"You make me sick!" Franka cuts it. Mungos, like an experienced detective, still watches over the closed door.

"But they forgot one thing," Skišul goes on. "It was July 27, Uprising Day. Police patrols all over. Because of the singing. And so they caught Marijan singing Marjane, Marjane on the hill of the same name. What a screw up—I mean destiny! They took him to the police station on charges of chauvinistic nationalism. On top of that he was a friar. Enemy of the people. But they didn't touch the Slovenes, because how could they be Croatian nationalists. The friar got sent to Goli for a while. To wash away his sins."

"Your uncle told you this, right?" asks the seasonal worker from Pag.

"That cousin of mine didn't screw over everybody here. Some of them did it to themselves. Or their destiny did it for them. Like with Marijan. They put him in with the worst. By then it was already a regular prison." Skišul lowered his voice now and unconsciously glanced toward the door behind which the man was relieving himself.

"Then they raped him. There on Goli. Fucked the man of God up his ass as if he was a harbor hooker."

"Ugh!" said Franka. She put a couple of bills down on the counter. "See you!" she told me and hurried toward the exit.

I tried to follow, but Mungos grabbed me by the arm. "We need to talk," he whispered, and Franka sprinted away toward the bus station on Palit, where she lived.

"The worst happened later. The police were screwing around

with him. Friar Marijan this, and Friar Marijan that, did you like your summer vacation, did you enjoy the entertainment program? All just to say his new nickname. But he didn't go mad, and he didn't hide, though he was having a hard time. His ass got completely ripped up. They had to stitch it at the clinic. But then later he began introducing himself like that. People stop him on the Riva and introduce him to their relatives, and he offers his hand and says, 'Nice to meet you, I'm Marijan!' And they get all ashamed, they say Friar Jerolim's our friend, Friar Jerolim baptized our little girl. But he always speaks about himself as Marijan. And so he stayed Marijan."

Only now, at the end of the story, as if he'd been waiting just for that, Marijan showed up, looking refreshed, with a gentle expression on his face, his hair wet and smoothed down with water as with brilliantine.

"Finally," said Mungos, as if all the time we'd been waiting just for him. We had in a way.

"Feel better?" asks Skišul, pretending to be worried about the godly man's health.

Mungos whispers to me, "I can't listen to him anymore! Let's go take a leak!"

So we go where the friar has just come from, as if making a pilgrimage to his shit. The police employee politely lets me go first through the door then positions himself above the urinal next to me. The idyllic solidarity of pissing.

"We have to talk about something. It's serious!" he says. "A tape showed up and I want you to get it."

"What tape?"

"The Match Girl's. She fucked in front of the camera, and now they're dealing it around the island."

"Why should I get it?"

"Well! It's your assignment. The guys from Rijeka told me

it's crucial. Some conclusion, eh? Of course it's crucial, but no one will sell it to a cop. Get it?"

"So they'll sell it to me?"

"Fuck! That's probably what it's for. To be sold. I only want to know who the men in the film are. And who played Fellini behind the camera?"

We pissed in silence for a while. The words from the bar reached us. Quite a lot of words and quite clearly. I realized Marijan had heard every word from here, that he'd met himself face to face all over again above the open toilet bowl, as in a mirror, and deliberately waited until the end of Skišul's lecture so as not to put him in an awkward situation. Maybe even because he wanted those of us who hadn't known to hear the story. I found it awful that all these years every morning Marijan had been putting on his name like a hair-shirt, as if doing penance. And all of us who called him by it had become his torturers without knowing it.

"Did you know about Marijan?" I ask.

"No," answers Mungos, shaking the remaining drops from his best friend and zipping his fly. "Luka invited us to his restaurant tonight. You, me, and Marijan. Says he has some information."

"Listen," I say, unsure if I want to say what I'm about to say or if this concerns me at all, "it crossed my mind while this guy from Pag was talking. The friars do taxidermy. They've stuffed all the sharks caught here in the last fifty years."

"So?"

"Ranko said the friars had raped the kid. Maybe he actually saw something else?"

"Ranko is a malingerer and full of shit," said Mungos, pausing to think. "You mean the friars dug her out and prep'd her. Why would they do that?"

"I don't know. Maybe there's something special about her for them. Ask Marijan!"

"I don't want to. If he knew something, he'd tell me."

"Are you sure?"

"No, fuck it!"

We went out to the others.

4 CIGARETTE LIGHTERS

Marijan's prickly name caused discomfort at first. Because we didn't know how to address him, and he was quiet. Almost all the way to Luka's restaurant. Until he finally said, "Those figs screwed me up!"

Strange, to then he'd never used swear words. As if what we'd learned about the origin of his name now gave us the right to look into that part of his soul as well.

"I stuffed my face with green figs up there above Faggot's Point."

This created a shock, and Mungos stopped. "Fuck, you're a friar, and you go to the nudist beach."

"Yeah. I guess I can tell you. I draw."

"The nudists?"

"Close your mouth, Fero? Nudism is a completely heavenly situation. Especially now that the tourists have gone."

"So you draw them?" asks Mungos.

"Sketch. I paint later. I found the fig tree there. I ate its fruit and thought about its leaves. About the Fall of Man. It all began with leaves. With hiding."

"Civilization began like that, Friar Marijan," I say.

"Yes. Civilization. But when people start hiding, it's not

good. And on this island there's too much hiding."

"What are you trying say?" asks Mungos.

"That we're not honest!"

"Friar Marijan," I say, wanting to somehow interrupt the ticklish conversation. "This thing with Mirna? Is it the first time something like that has happened? I mean a child stolen from its grave?"

"You see," says Marijan in Mungos' direction. "Fero thinks I know something. But I know nothing, like you two."

Talking in the restroom, I had obviously forgotten sound travels in both directions and if someone inside can hear people talking outside, people outside can hear someone talking inside. Terribly embarrassed, I say, "I'm sorry, Friar Marijan! I only remembered those stuffed animals."

"If you don't know," said Mungos in a conciliatory tone. "Maybe the brothers know? The ones with Land Rovers."

"Now I'm going to tell you everything I know," he said, obviously addressing Mungos. "So you don't have to pussyfoot around me anymore. Renata wanted to get over with the First Communion before the kid's hair fell out. So they could have normal photos. We squeezed her in with the older children. And the kids came to confession. You know what kids say at confession: 'I stole a chocolate bar at the store....' But when it was Mirna's turn, I saw she was already weak, she began talking about something kids usually don't talk about."

"About what?"

"About people. Not about her sins. About other people's sins. She had enough of her own as well. The gossip around the island had it that she liked taking people's things."

"She was stealing?" I asked.

"Not exactly stealing. She just liked taking things. A kleptomaniac."

"What did she tell you about other people?" Mungos asked.

"For example, that you tortured animals. That you had camps for ants and flies. That you baked a live mouse in clay."

"Fuck!" said Mungos. His old sins obviously shocked him. But he recovered from it quickly. "That's nothing new, half the island knows I tortured animals. Fuck it. Now I'm torturing people. It's my job."

"Yes. But children usually don't talk like that. At confession they talk only about themselves. By the end she started shaking. I opened the curtain. I thought she was having some kind of a seizure. When she calmed down, she began speaking in some strange language."

"What language?" Mungos said through his teeth.

"It sounded like Romanian," the friar answered.

Luka welcomed us at the entrance to his restaurant, under the large sign SUNČANI SAT, 'The Sundial,' in stylish letters made of thick copper. I watched as he shook hands affectionately with Marijan. He took Marijan's palm in his little hands and held them closed for quite a while. Until the man of God grew uncomfortable by the other ingratiating himself so much. Because in past times, actually ever since he'd opened the restaurant some ten years before, Luka had been very suspicious about everything associated with the Church. And all that time the only thing connected to the clergy here was the stuffed shark in the main room. He kindly let us into the restaurant.

"Here, have some pear brandy for starters!" he said.

On an old-fashioned chest of drawers, right next to the entrance, stood a darkened alpaca tray with a few shot glasses filled with the clear white liquid, Prior William's. We toasted our health, all four of us, locking eyes. Then Luka led us through the half-empty room to the table under the stuffed shark where Franka and I had recently gorged ourselves on farm-raised sea bass.

"Make yourselves comfortable," he said. "I'm still busy. I'll sit down with you later."

I confess Luka treated us like kings. It's a pity Marijan couldn't eat because of his diarrhea. First came prosciutto and cheese from Pag. Then some excellent fish soup with a few large shrimp swimming in it here and there. After that octopus salad and salmon steaks in a white horse-radish sauce. This was the middle course. For the main they served a four-pound sea bass, grilled over a wood fire. All this time we were more or less quiet because the dishes kept coming one after another very quickly.

At last, stirring his coffee with a short plastic spoon, Mungos said, "By God, that was good."

"You can tell he wants something," said Marijan. He obviously meant Luka.

I watched as he worked. He stood by the bar, or in the main room's corner, next to the large open fireplace, and observed the tables. All slim and small, with short light hair, he bore his age well. He too had turned forty, but his face, when you watched it from a distance, still had the childish look he was famous for. Once you came nearer, it turned a little grotesque because of his aging skin. All together it resembled a mannequin whose exterior had cracked. He moved very skillfully and responded to his guests' every wish. His was one of the few restaurants still open, so Luka was careful to gather the remains of this summer's poor harvest.

When he noticed we'd finished our dinner, he came to our table and said, "Now we can move to my apartment. I've got some good cognac."

For the second time that evening he led us through the main dining room into a small hall and then into something that looked like a cross between a living room and the interior of a saloon from a western. There was a mini bar made of dark oak, a table and chairs, and a small liquor cabinet, all of the same wood. The walls were covered in green carpet. A few imitation oil lamps with yellow glass shades suspended from the walls. And on the wall above the fireplace stood Luka's collection of cigarette lighters. We sat around the table. He poured the cognac.

"First, I have a request for Friar Marijan," he said.

The friar fidgeted in his chair a little. He understood it was time to pay for the eel, the sea bass, and the shrimp in the soup. And the bottle of Plavac. Which he hadn't even tasted.

"My wife has a niece in Rijeka. Her name's Aranka. She's nineteen, she used to visit us in summer. Well, she's getting married…"

"And doesn't have all the sacraments," Friar Marijan finished his sentence. "No problem."

"She was baptized. She needs the rest. It's awfully embarrassing. To scrounge like this. But my wife. Every day. She doesn't let me live."

"No problem," Marijan repeated. He just wanted him to stop.

"Fuck, you've been whining for as long as I can remember," said Mungos, getting up from the table to look at the cigarette lighters on the wall. "Ask him nicely and that's it. He'll give her the Communion and everything else she needs."

Luka seemed satisfied.

"I'll get the cards so we can play some Belot."

"But first, what was it you wanted to tell us about that other girl."

"Ah, the Romanian?" Luka said, pretending he'd forgotten. He did this to infuriate Mungos. "I think I know who has the tape!"

We stopped talking. Only faint noise from the restaurant could be heard, porcelain clinking against porcelain as plates were collected, chairs scraping against the floor.

"Who?" hissed Mungos.

"Bobo! I don't know who he bought it from or why."

"The writer?"

"You saw the tape?"

"No. He told me."

"Will you search his house?" asked Marijan. It seemed the cognac had brought him back to life.

"No. Maybe it would be better if Fero took it from him somehow."

"How?" I said.

"Easy! Franka knows Bobo well. He could invite you for dinner."

"And then I'd sneak around his house. It'd be much easier if you…"

"And stupider!" whispered Mungos. "I don't want to bring the guys from Rijeka into this for now. At least until we see what's on it. Besides, it's not stealing. We'd impound it officially anyhow as a part of the investigation."

Meanwhile Luka was pouring another round. Then he brought a deck of cards and we started playing. We hadn't played together like this for a very long time. Then Marijan got sick again. He stood up suddenly, almost knocked the chair down, and flew toward the toilet.

"Figs again," Mungos tossed in, staring at his cards. He looked at them as if he could see our destiny. Luka got nervous. He'd never seen a friar with diarrhea. Maybe it even insulted his new found religion, which he'd given up for the restaurant license.

"Did you hear?" he said. "Some strange kids have shown up

on the island."

"What kids?" asked Mungos. He couldn't hide his surprise.

"The other night I'm driving toward Supetarska Draga. Moon's out, Luna shining like it's the middle of the day. And right on that curve, up there where you first see Draga, I see two kids by the road. A boy and a girl. But it's three A.M., not a soul around. The horror."

"We only saw a girl," I said. "Franka and I. When we went to Sahara to have a swim. Franka thought it was Mirna."

"Why didn't you tell me this?" Mungos asked. It seemed his police ego was a little hurt. But his much tougher civilian one was still intact.

"Because you'd think I'd gone nuts," I said.

We were silent, sitting like that for a while. Then Luka got up and went toward the hall. "I've got to check the dining room."

Mungos and I were alone at the table, sipping our drinks. The cognac had warmed my lungs and spine, which is how it is with good drinks. Others only affect the stomach. Meanwhile Mungos glanced at his cards, propped on the table in the shape of a fan, then put them down again, spreading them so all I could see was their backs. He got up and approached the lighter collection.

"Fero," he said. "Come see this!"

Luka's lighter collection stood on a large square waterproof plywood board with a teak veneer. The lighters were fastened to the small metal sheet mounts with white rubber bands. The whole thing looked very impressive. I suddenly recognized some of the lighters.

For example a Ronson with a gilded locomotive imprint. A railroader's lighter. There was a date on it. Maybe somebody's father's jubilee, after he'd worked for the railroad and died from

TB, but before the final showdown with his lung cavities he'd given this gift to his student son. All polished, there weren't any blood stains on it anymore. Not from the TB, or anything else. There was a Zippo with a stylized drawing of a bicycle. Cheep stuff, no gild or date on it. It couldn't have been a present. Bought in a hurry at some railway station before a departure. The blood had been removed from it long ago. But there must have been some under this shiny metal. Because Luka had taken the lighters as trophies, the spoils of war, right while we were kicking in the head and body.

Everything would begin at our usual meeting place, at the edge of the park, in front of the entrance to Hotel Istria. Mungos' war cry, "Let's go beat some faggots, kids!" would attract a nice cohort of island teenagers armed with brass knuckles, sticks, and boots with pointy tips. Then we'd move into the park. Luka always went first, completely alone. With his boyish face and blonde curls he was an attractive target for the homosexuals who gathered around the floral display in the center of the park. He always had an unlit cigarette in the corner of his mouth. He'd approach the lonely walker, who, let's say, watched him lustfully, and then twitter, his little voice breaking: "Please, have you fire?" Like he was hitting on our English teacher at a make-up exam. The man would then take out a lighter and light his cigarette. The bright yellow flash would illuminate their faces for a moment. That's exactly what I remember most—the faces.

I gradually connect them with the lighters Luka picked up from the ground later when the man was down, lying in a pool of blood. Because right at the moment the lighter flashed and Luka saw the slobbering face after his ass, he'd strike impeccably between the legs. The flame would then die out with the same precision as the foot had met resistance in the man's genitals. Then the rest of us, hidden in the bushes until then, would attack. We'd strike without order, even pushing each other to get the feel of crushing the human flesh under us. The thing that always amazed me was how the victims usually stopped yelling after a few blows. They were horror struck and seemed to somehow withdrew into themselves or pretend they weren't in their bodies but in some higher spheres, like the ancient Christians. Silence was the worst because blows generated their own sounds. Gasps, the smacking of lips, the loud noise of toothless mouths swallowing blood, occasional cries. Maybe even a flash of light for a moment, which was Luka testing the lighter or studying it in its own light.

The gold Ronson seemed especially tragic. It was surely quite valuable. Maybe a present from his mother. Very feminine. With an engraved monogram JR. Had mother already known about her son's homosexuality? Doubtless if she'd given him such a feminine gift. Or maybe it was a present from an old lover. Tasteful elegance and simplicity. Was JR just a monogram or was it a nickname. Junior? Wealth, the love of beautiful things, tolerance. All of it would suddenly fall under our feet. The lighter belonged to a young man whose spine we had terminally injured. He had left the island some twenty days later, dragging his foot. And no one had answered for it, though everybody on the island knew who was beating up the homosexuals. The police could have found out in half an hour if they'd wanted to.

I ask Mungos, who has also focused on the lighters how come they didn't arrest us.

"You should ask the city council. Your old man could explain it to you too, if he were alive."

"What has my old man got to do with it?"

"He was in the organization too."

"What organization?"

"The major big shots on the island. The unofficial authorities. The retired generals who built their weekend houses here and have hotels moved because they block their view of the sea. Mostly those guys."

"I don't understand," I say, as if Goli Otok isn't my father's only sin, if he really ever had any, since he was only the psychologist there, a doctor-scribbler and distributor of God's tranquilizers. Sent by the Secretariat of Internal Affairs.

"Development strategy," says Mungos, "five-year plan, ten-year plan. This thing with faggots was the first time all our eminences reached an agreement."

But I'm looking at him as if he's speaking Chinese. What eminences is he talking about? I know only about the éminence grise. He sees I'm confused, so he says, "Priests and commies. They agreed at a historical meeting at St. Euphemia they couldn't allow the homosexuals' invasion of the island. It had a negative influence on the youth. Then Svemir Tadić said the youth were the ones who should settle that score. Unofficially of course."

Realizing the most powerful manifestation of our freedom had actually come as a directive from a joint political-spiritual center could not touch me anymore. I'm now immune to such revelations. I only snicker at the fact that I had slipped by the walls of the reformatory and juvie without a scratch, so now I'm looking at the lighters with my past clean, at least in an administrative sense, spotless. Almost.

If dice are whores, cards are a brothel. So many perverse com-
binations in a deck, each of which can turn bad. That's why
we mumble, hiss, swear, and cry out Jesus' name. Like Tomo
at soccer. Marijan returned from the incriminating little room
somehow cleansed, and Luka brought his day's takings, obviously satisfied with the successful post-season dinner. We've
gradually forgotten about the lighters and are now playing for
anyone's sake, for a glance, a curse, a compliment. Just not for
money, though this room is notorious on the island. It has
been serving as an illegal casino for years. In these fifteen odd
years the room has digested all kinds of things, from a plastic
fishing boat that belonged to Tomo's father, to two or three Yu-
gos, in the time before the flood, to our house here, which my
father supposedly lost one evening after he'd eaten too much
cod. It's interesting how everybody put the two together natu-
rally, almost as if there was some mystical connection between
them, the loss and the cod.

After a night at the poker table in this room, he came out
very angry, supposedly as if he had some kind of fever. He
vomited three times on his way home, came to the door, but
was so beside himself he couldn't find the key. He wanted to
get the deed for the house. He rummaged through his pockets
but couldn't find the key anywhere. In the end, swearing up a
storm, he picked up the doormat, carried it back, and threw
it here on the table, in front of his shocked poker partners. It
stood for his house.

He lost of course. That sobered him up. But supposedly
none of the players from that evening had even thought of later
disputing his right to the house. His loss was somehow fictional,

ansfer of title. Actually without any transfer
ce value. In the morning he dragged himself
ely broken. I often imagine him like that. He's
a Srednja Street, the doormat under his arm, as
bought it at the market and not lost his home. The
orning sun's drawing yellow Lego blocks on the worn
es, and maybe he's crying. Maybe the bitter melody
ballad "House of the Rising Sun" is in the background.
now at the entrance to the house, he finds the key at once,
it seems chance has given him a very warm hug. He puts
the doormat back in its place that morning. It's still there, even
today, as if it outliving him from spite.

My father encountered that doormat once again, face
to face, like in a duel. It happened on his return from the
Stubičke Toplice rehabilitation center after his right leg had
been amputated. Supported by the paramedics, who held him
under the armpits, he bent down with difficulty to straighten it because it was crooked. He knew he'd never again wipe
his foot on it because with the crutches, that was almost impossible. But it probably seemed to him that by straightening the mat he was straightening all the curves that had come
our way.

I should have realized long before that they would cut
my old man's leg off. Back then when we all lived in Zagreb,
whenever my mother washed the colored clothes on Saturday
mornings, a few of my father's socks would disappear. She'd
put them, let's say, in pairs into the washer, but when she'd
hang them on the line in back after the hot rinse and spin
cycles, some would be missing. Every time a few disappeared,
so those without partners hung down strange and all alone.
There hadn't yet been any word about the sugar, gangrene, and
amputation. Years later, I read a book about pens disappearing

We almost ran across the open space alongside the little port and hurried on toward the monastery. But as we reached the main road to Kampor, Marijan told us to wait in front of the entrance. This meant the monastery wasn't our destination. The wind was beating along the monastery walls, and we heard the sound of branches cracking and a window slamming shut. Marmalade jars and other handy vases were falling off the graves at the Kampor cemetery. It was getting creepier all the time. Then I saw there were no Land Rovers in the parking lot. I wanted to tell Mungos, but he was sleeping standing up, propped against the wall.

Marijan came back pretty quickly, still in his civilian clothes, carrying something under his jacket. We woke Mungos and went down the road. Not far from the monastery I saw the Bura had knocked down one of the gray citizens and thought how we'd almost forgotten about them. We were on the high ground and could see the dark valley in which there'd been an Italian concentration camp during the occupation.

We stopped only after reaching Kampor hospital — several shabby, oblong buildings, resembling camp barracks, surrounded by coniferous forest. Kampor was an asylum and a kind of vacation home for the incurably mentally ill. Their occasional penetration into town would make the town's people happy, but the institution itself was not at all cheerful. Marijan didn't lead us toward the stone guard house at the entrance. Instead we turned down by the fence to the southwest. A strong gust struck us again, and a cloud of pine needles hit me in the face. Sand came with it. I covered my eyes with my hands and rubbed them to provoke tears and get the sand out. I knew well how to fight against the wind here. When I opened them, Mungos and Marijan were gone. I was all alone by the fence

"She's calmed down a bit," Mungos whispered. "But you'll see when she starts."

A man in a Franciscan habit was sitting at the table on the right. A huge tape recorder was on the table, and he had headphones on. He was just changing the tape. Next to him, on a man-sized stand was a video camera and a small spotlight that was the source of that strange light I'd seen from outside. There were more people dressed in Franciscan habits, two hospital attendants, Edigio Franjina, the director of the psychiatric asylum, and a nun. One of the Franciscans was performing an exorcism. When he sprinkled her with holy water, the woman began jerking even more frantically, crying out something. The man with the tape recorder said: "September 17th, 1992. Milanka Krstinić, one hour after midnight! Friar Serafim."

The friar sprinkled holy water over her again, and the woman began jerking as if it were live coals. Everyone in the room started mumbling prayers. The sound the woman made was similar to a little child crying. She imitated it very well. Then the friar began reading the Gospel: "Then Jesus was led by the Spirit into the desert to be tempted by the devil. After fasting forty days and forty nights, he was hungry. The tempter came to him and said, 'If you are the Son of God, tell these stones to become bread.'"

As the friar read the Gospel, the people standing around mumbled prayers, and the voice from the woman's stomach grew stronger. Now it resembled the screaming of a cat in heat.

Then the exorcist began reading the Psalms: "O Lord, thou hast brought up my soul from the grave: thou hast kept me alive, that I should not go down to the pit."

The woman screamed. Blood mixed with saliva issued from her mouth. She had obviously hurt herself with her teeth. This

We almost ran across the open space alongside the little port and hurried on toward the monastery. But as we reached the main road to Kampor, Marijan told us to wait in front of the entrance. This meant the monastery wasn't our destination. The wind was beating along the monastery walls, and we heard the sound of branches cracking and a window slamming shut. Marmalade jars and other handy vases were falling off the graves at the Kampor cemetery. It was getting creepier all the time. Then I saw there were no Land Rovers in the parking lot. I wanted to tell Mungos, but he was sleeping standing up, propped against the wall.

Marijan came back pretty quickly, still in his civilian clothes, carrying something under his jacket. We woke Mungos and went down the road. Not far from the monastery I saw the Bura had knocked down one of the gray citizens and thought how we'd almost forgotten about them. We were on the high ground and could see the dark valley in which there'd been an Italian concentration camp during the occupation.

We stopped only after reaching Kampor hospital—several shabby, oblong buildings, resembling camp barracks, surrounded by coniferous forest. Kampor was an asylum and a kind of vacation home for the incurably mentally ill. Their occasional penetration into town would make the town's people happy, but the institution itself was not at all cheerful. Marijan didn't lead us toward the stone guard house at the entrance. Instead we turned down by the fence to the southwest. A strong gust struck us again, and a cloud of pine needles hit me in the face. Sand came with it. I covered my eyes with my hands and rubbed them to provoke tears and get the sand out. I knew well how to fight against the wind here. When I opened them, Mungos and Marijan were gone. I was all alone by the fence of the mental institution, which wasn't pleasant. I called out once, softly, then again, more loudly. But the wind carried my voice away.

Then I heard faint screaming from somewhere, like the mating of cats, or a child crying.

6 ANDREA

Standing in the wind by the psychiatric hospital fence, listening to sometimes louder and sometimes fainter screams carried on the gusts of the Bura, I remembered Mirna. And her Romanian. On this island with its four noons, during the summer season four foreign languages were most often heard: German, Italian, Slovenian, and Czech. And sometimes English. But where had she heard Romanian? This thought stayed with me as I made my way through the thicket along the fence, looking for Marijan and Mungos. I forced myself in the direction of the screams. At intervals they'd grow quiet. Then I'd listen to the wind alone. Moving on I found a hole in the fence and entered the hospital park. At one moment I heard a scream very clearly, but then everything was quiet again. I couldn't discern where it was coming from, so I crouched by one of the pavilions, my back against the wall. And waited.

The next scream broke perfectly clear from a small single-storey pavilion at the end of the park. One of the windows was lit by a strange, white light that differered from the yellowish tone of the other hospital windows. I went toward it. At that moment I caught sight of a man's silhouette coming out of the pavilion, trying to light a cigarette. He struck a match several times, and the flames disturbed by the wind sporadically lit his face. When the screams from the inside grew louder, the man, still smoking, leaned with his whole body against the wall. He threw his head back, as if resting from something. I paused, not knowing whether to approach or not, and then another man appeared next to him. He said something. I recognized Mungos' voice and went up.

"Where the fuck have you been?" he said, standing next to the guy with the cigarette. Something had sobered him up. "I've just told him to tell you we're inside if you come."

The man with the cigarette nodded. His eyes told me I should be prepared for anything.

Mungos took me into the pavilion. As we entered I smelled the smoke and damp from the walls. We walked down the central corridor, empty rooms on both sides. Doors had been removed here and there. Meanwhile the screams quieted, and white light reached out from the room at the end of the corridor.

"What's going on?" I whispered.

"When we get in, don't ask anything. Just stand by the wall."

We reached the door. The smell of candles hit me. The room was quite big—obviously it had once served as a waiting room. There were many people standing or sitting along the walls, and in the middle was a bed with an older woman lying on it. She was tied up with leather straps, and I noticed her hands were jerking frantically. It seemed she was unconscious. I met Marijan's eyes. He held a cross in his hand. Then I noticed other people held rosaries or candles. Several candles were burning on the floor around the bed. Next to the woman's head there was a small altar, improvised on an old-fashioned dresser. There was a crucifix, a picture of the Blessed Virgin with Jesus, a chalice, and two lit candles.

"She's calmed down a bit," Mungos whispered. "But you'll see when she starts."

A man in a Franciscan habit was sitting at the table on the right. A huge tape recorder was on the table, and he had headphones on. He was just changing the tape. Next to him, on a man-sized stand was a video camera and a small spotlight that was the source of that strange light I'd seen from outside. There were more people dressed in Franciscan habits, two hospital attendants, Edigio Franjina, the director of the psychiatric asylum, and a nun. One of the Franciscans was performing an exorcism. When he sprinkled her with holy water, the woman began jerking even more frantically, crying out something. The man with the tape recorder said: "September 17th, 1992. Milanka Krstinić, one hour after midnight! Friar Serafim."

The friar sprinkled holy water over her again, and the woman began jerking as if it were live coals. Everyone in the room started mumbling prayers. The sound the woman made was similar to a little child crying. She imitated it very well. Then the friar began reading the Gospel: "Then Jesus was led by the Spirit into the desert to be tempted by the devil. After fasting forty days and forty nights, he was hungry. The tempter came to him and said, 'If you are the Son of God, tell these stones to become bread.'"

As the friar read the Gospel, the people standing around mumbled prayers, and the voice from the woman's stomach grew stronger. Now it resembled the screaming of a cat in heat.

Then the exorcist began reading the Psalms: "O Lord, thou hast brought up my soul from the grave: thou hast kept me alive, that I should not go down to the pit."

The woman screamed. Blood mixed with saliva issued from her mouth. She had obviously hurt herself with her teeth. This was the sign for the exorcist to begin. "So you have abandoned our holy church. You have committed foul deeds in this garden, in this vineyard. Answer me!"

The woman began to wheeze. She seemed to be choking, and the convulsions in her body intensified.

"Answer me! Confess your filth and your lies!"

Words started coming from the woman's mouth. It wasn't the high-pitched voice of a child but seemed more like a man's. Or the hoarse voice of a woman imitating male speech.

"It is I!"

"How old are you?"

"Ninety."

"Are you a woman or a man?"

The strapped woman began laughing viciously. "Guess!" she said. "Jesus' milk on you!"

"Have you committed those foul deeds?"

"Foul deeds?! You shit of a syphilitic child!"

She kept laughing. More blood came out of her mouth.

"Have you done what you say you did?"

"Yes!"

"Against God, our Savior, and his mother the Blessed Virgin."

"Shove God up your ass! You butthole of a butthole!"

"The name! Who are you?"

"Shove the name up your ass, you butthole of a butthole!"

At that moment the friar began reciting the Psalms: "O Lord, how many are my foes! Many are rising against me!"

"Shove that up your ass, you pig in heat! A dog is fucking your mother!"

"Many are saying of me, there is no help for him in God."

"Eenie, meenie, miney mo, catch a dead man by the toe…"

"But thou, O Lord, art a shield about me, my glory, and the lifter of my head."

"If it falls off, let it go. Eenie, meenie, miney moe!"

Then everyone began praying together: "Our Father..."

The woman's body jerked. I heard her releasing gas.

The friar went on, "The name! Tell us your name!"

"She's been farting all the time," Mungos whispered.

The woman was wheezing. It seemed she was choking, "Aaarrrrgh! Aaarrrrgh!"

"The name! Say the name!"

The demon spoke with a horrible grimace on its face: "Andrea!"

"Your name's Andrea? Andrea what?"

"Andrea! Baldo, Andrea!"

Then there was silence. One could hear only the turning of the recording device reels and the rustle of the tape. Having heard the name, the nun crossed herself and stormed out of the room. The strapped woman fell into something that looked like sleep.

7 COUNCIL

In his office, where the window surely offered a nice view of the Italian concentration camp memorial during the day, Edigio Franjina occupied himself with the tapes. On the desk were several recordings of exorcisms performed on Milanka Krstinić at different times since the beginning of September. The tape he was rewinding released incoherent, accelerated voices. Mungos and I sat in the worn out brown leather armchairs that stood before the desk. A little to the side was a set of bamboo chairs darkened by weather and use, obviously transferred here from somebody's terrace. Friar Serafim sat as well, chatting quietly with Marijana, the nun, who'd just brought a tray with juice and coffee. It was well after two in the morning.

"Andrea is an Italian male name," said Edigio Franjina, rewinding the tape. Every now and then he stopped the recorder to hear where the tape was. I didn't miss the fact that the nun had crossed herself every time she heard the name.

"Andrea Baldo was an officer down in the concentration camp during the war," the director of island psychiatry went on.

"What did he do?" I asked, impatient.

"He took advantage of little children. He'd bribe them with food. Afterward he'd kill them by injecting gasoline. But he wasn't alone…"

The exorcist jumped in. "Often a man is possessed by more than one demon," said Friar Serafim in Croatian with a noticeable Italian accent. "The age is right."

"I don't understand one thing," I told Edigio. "How come you allow all this?"

"What?"

"Maybe I misunderstood something, but I can hardly put medicine and exorcism together."

"They're closer than you think. Mrs. Krstinić was seven in 1943. It is possible she remembers. If not directly, then she heard stories. She's been in treatment here for years, and she's the only islander of all our patients."

Meanwhile Marijan gave me a sign with his eyebrows to stop the discussion. As a doctor for the dead, I had to accept the explanations of the doctor for the soul. Nobody in medicine understands what psychiatrists say anyhow.

"There's no doubt that Milanka Krstinić is a schizophrenic," said Friar Serafim. "The diagnosis is not the problem."

"Then what is?"

"Listen! The woman's been in treatment for years, but only recently has she begun showing signs of prior possession. And this is different from her medical diagnosis."

"First there's prior possession," the nun explained. She was sitting next to Friar Serafim. "It also has stages, like illnesses. The prior possessed person is not controlled by the demon yet, he resists, and the demon doesn't speak through him. There are sound and olfactory hallucinations."

"Most often the smell of feces," Marijan tossed in ironically. It was enough to make me think that the cause of his intestinal perturbations were not nudists' figs, but something else. Maybe cleansing agents.

"Excrement is usually connected with the demonic," Friar Serafim explained, without commenting on Marijan's irony. "And an exorcist must first cleanse himself thoroughly."

I thought Friar Marijan had cleansed himself more than thoroughly. He'd been in the john for a good third of the time we'd spent together that evening.

"She is already in the second stage," the nun went on. "This is the possession stage. The demon has complete possession of her and she is under its control. This can be compared to a siege of a medieval castle. It has surrounded the castle, it sends armies to the walls, blocks the supply of food and water. But those inside still resist. Only when the enemy breaks into the castle can we speak about a successful siege. The demonic army that was outside is now inside."

"I'm more interested in the other demon," said Mungos, who seemed to have suddenly woken up from a long sleep.

"Wait!" said the clinic director, fumbling with the recorder.

"I've been looking for this place all the time."

"Had you let me put the needles into her, we would've heard everything," said the nun.

"Needles?" I said. The thought of porn film piercing occurred to me.

"If you cause it pain, the demon speaks in its own voice. And its own language. Greek, Coptic, Aramaic."

"Demons feel pain?" I asked. I seemed to be the only one here without professional demonic knowledge. Except for maybe Mungos, who was dozing in the armchair, waiting for them to bring up the thing that interested him.

"Strange, isn't it?" said Friar Serafim. "But then again true. Although they're a spiritual category, the demons feel pain. Because pain is also a matter of spirit. Or, if you want, electricity. If there are no centers for pain in the brain, there is no pain. There are people whose pain centers have been destroyed and they can't feel it. I know of a girl who didn't know about pain until she was five, when she accidentally pressed her hand against a red-hot stove ring. She turned around only after she'd smelled the burning flesh. Unlike her, demons feel pain. However, only for a short time. That's the difference between us and them. If you cut a living being in half, it is impossible to put it back together again. A demon cut in half reattaches and renews itself immediately, like particles of air or water. When you cut the demon, it's like cutting into the sea. The spirit regains its old form. But during cutting or piercing, in that short moment, even the demon feels pain. Very intense pain. That's why the needles are used."

I looked at Doctor Egidio, and he looked back at me with a shrug. This thing with needles didn't please him either. Meanwhile I remembered the little rhyme I'd seen on the Imperial poster:

I cut women in two pieces,
Belly, legs, and white tights.
I cut bodies with a sharp saw
In the end they come out nice!

Now the simple ad lines took on new meaning. Nor could I forget Ranko's blabbing about saws. It seemed that saws on this island, like doormats, had become a strange constant.

Meanwhile the doctor for souls abandoned his recorder for a moment and began searching through some papers, clearly transcripts made from the tapes.

"On the twelfth, for example, this Mr. Andrea said that in the winter of '42 he had copulated with a newborn child. A woman had given birth on a bunk, and he took the baby still covered in blood, satisfied himself with it, and then washed it in ice cold water so it should die. Then he watched as the little child slowly faded away on its mother's breast."

"This guy was pretty unpleasant," said Mungos. "but why don't you give us what we came here for?"

Egidio messed around with the tape recorder while the rest of us were quiet. It seemed we'd exhausted the demon topic. We could hear the wind howling outside. The whole building shook from top to bottom. The windows and doors rattled, and unpleasant cold drafts penetrated into the room, lifting the papers from the table.

Egidio stopped the recorder. "Here! Listen!"

The same wheezing sound came from the recording, which obviously came from before the conversation with the demon. And the prayer of the people all around...

"There's one more! There's one more!" the woman yelled.

"What's it like? Tell us what it's like," said Friar Serafim, his voice disturbed.

The woman wheezed again, as if something within her wasn't letting her speak. Then, finally, stiffly, she enunciated: "Sad!"

Friar Serafim waved his hand and Egidio paused the tape. "Interesting," he said. "I've never heard anything like this."

More wheezing and screaming followed on the recording. We could hear her body jerking against the leather straps. Then suddenly she spoke, and her voice had changed. It was rather clear. "Little children rise from their graves, becoming an army."

These words made me reflect. I remembered the hopscotch and the little girl from Sahara. Besides, there was Luka's story about the boy and girl at the curve above Supetarska Draga. The woman's horrible wheezing gave me goose-bumps. Then she said, "The child's body is rotting under the stars!"

Mungos and Marijan listened attentively. Prayer could be heard above the woman's voice, "Our Father…"

"… on the island."

"What do you hear?" yelled Friar Serafim.

"Little worms and ants, and the wind."

Again the loud Our Father muffled her words.

Doctor Egidio turned off the recorder. "You can't hear anything after this!"

"It's nothing," said Marijan. "The mad woman's raving."

"Don't neglect this," Friar Serafim said in Mungos' direction. "The possessed usually have the gift of knowing something they otherwise couldn't know. Besides, that's one of the main symptoms of demonic possession. In a number of cases their words have been true."

"Like this?" I asked. It seemed pretty unbelievable to me.

"Exactly like this!"

"It would mean the kid's body is out in the open," said Marijan. "Under the stars. That's what it probably means."

"The dogs arrive tomorrow," said Mungos. "If she's in the open, they'll find her."

Mungos was the first to stand, and we said goodbye. Outside day was breaking, the Bura had died down. We could even hear the birds. The whole landscape, all things and people, was colored with the bluish light of dawn. We zipped our jackets and dove into the sharp air. Only Marijan fumbled around with his own zipper.

"Why are you wearing civilian clothes, Marijan?" asked Mungos, as if he'd just noticed.

"Because I don't think much of exorcism. I didn't want to participate in it as a priest."

"But still you cleansed yourself?" I said.

"That was their condition. Now you've seen the show. What do you think?"

We started down the road toward town.

"I'm surprised by Egidio. An inspection from the Ministry of Health could take away his license."

"What license? He's looked after like a Griffon Vulture from Cres. Do you know why he does this?"

"No."

"He's writing his doctorate. About schizophrenia and exorcism. The influence of exorcism on psychoses. Something like that."

"And the patients are his guinea pigs… I'd report him to the medical association."

"Don't do it before we finish this thing with the kid," said Mungos.

"It concerns you too. It's pure torture. And illegal imprisonment."

"I don't give a flying fuck about that," said Mungos.

We were quiet for a while. It took a couple of moments of silence for our raised voices to disperse in the wind. Then I said, "Listen, it crossed my mind. The thing about cutting the deceased in half. That's maybe out of the fear of demons and not the council tomb."

"What do you mean?" asked Marijan. He seemed taken aback.

"Well, you heard Friar Serafim. The demon cut it in half immediately reattaches itself. Maybe that's why they cut the Americans in half. To see if they'll grow back together or not. They even put them in those little boxes so there's no way they could become whole again."

"You're sick, Fero," said Marijan. "In that case my shepherd's work here is not worth more than my diarrhea last night."

None of us said anything more. We allowed the morning to swallow us up in silence.

8 A CHARRED CRICKET AND A GOLD BOX

When we reached the monastery, we lifted one of those metal sculptures that had astonished the whole town the morning before back onto its stand. The wind from the night before had knocked it down.

"So nobody knows what this thing is, right?" Marijan asked Mungos, who was wiping his hands with a hanky as if to decontaminate himself, just in case, from the tin monster.

"Maybe they put them here to mark demons?" I said. No one laughed.

Marijan only said, "Shut up, will you!"

"Serafim's right about one thing, though," I went on. "I wouldn't ignore this thing with the demons. There are too many coincidences. I heard from one of the people praying in the room that Satan always comes with a black dog."

"Sure, and a black cat, and sulfur, and the smell of burning, sometimes he has a goat in tow, and sometimes he has a goat foot and smells of urine and feces." Marijan wasn't convinced the devil could appear. With some agitation he went on, "Now I'll take you to the library and show you what kind of devil this is."

He led us to the library through the empty church and the atrium, just as he had a couple of days before when we'd watched the Land Rovers. He sat us down on the small wooden benches the friars used to reach the books on the top shelves. There was Testen's famous fir wood desk all covered in paint. Magazines and newspapers lay on it. There were copies of Glas Koncila and Kana, but I also noticed some secular news-papers—Vjesnik, Arena, Večernji List. He began searching through them nervously.

"I saw it here, somewhere... from last week."

"What are you looking for?" I asked.

"That devil of yours!"

And then he found it. He opened a magazine to the cen-ter and showed us a color photograph spread over both pages. We saw several massacred corpses lying in the grass, one next to another. Their faces were unrecognizable because the photo wasn't very sharp, but we could tell some had had their eyes cut out. Something was printed in tiny white letters in the bot-tom corner of the page. It had happened in Banija. The army had raided a village before the civilians had managed to retreat. They'd caught a woman in labor and killed her together with the newborn. The baby was all bloody, its umbilical cord still attached. One of the soldiers, supposedly, had had his picture taken just after he'd slit the mother's throat. But that photo wasn't included.

"What do you say now?" Friar Marijan said, as if he'd proven something important to us.

"What should I say?" I replied. It wasn't exactly clear what he wanted to show.

He raised the magazine. "The hospital subscribes to this too. You think they don't read this there? A madman absorbs everything around him, then he feeds his hallucinations with it."

Logical but I wasn't completely convinced. We left Marijan with the blind corpses. He could say prayers for them now, maybe throw in a couple for us. Mungos and I went toward Škver. I thought after all these demonic apparitions a walk by the sea would do us good. The air was cold and sharp. I noticed the smell of summer was giving way to that of fall. The fragrance of the pines was no longer as intense, and the sweet scent of the sea had somehow changed. I used to associate that with the beginning of the school year.

"Do you smell that?" I said. "Like school."

I thought some old sentiments couldn't hurt at the moment. But Mungos responded in his usual way.

"Did I tell you Vjeko became the director of the dog cemetery in Rijeka?"

"Director?" I said, thinking after all the most important thing was getting promoted. At a dog cemetery or wherever. We called him Truli, which meant something like "rotten." Mungos had launched the story that dogs loved him so much because of his bad breath. As soon as a dog got near him, it started wagging its tail because it could smell the half-rotten fish, potato or goulash on his breath. The inclination was reciprocal: he began loving dogs back. This surely had a lot to do with his choice of college. I remember his mother, when he graduated in vet medicine up in Zagreb, had talked all over the island about her Vjeko becoming a doctor. She didn't mention dogs. It was sad to watch her show the photo of Vjeko receiving his doctor's degree to everybody. Behind her back people said there was a cow bone — his most important instrument — sticking out the pocket of his borrowed suit. Even my old man said it. I'd just graduated in medicine. He couldn't know that in the years to come I'd become a doctor for the dead. And now both of us dealt with the dead, Vjeko with dogs, I with people. Cosmic justice.

"He treats police dogs for the whole Rijeka region," Mungos said. "He called me up yesterday and said they were coming. They're going to find her, no doubt about it. Especially if she's out in the open."

But I was interested in something else. "The thing with the Match Girl, what do you think, is that a ritual of some kind?"

"Why?"

"The injuries are strange. If it were an animal, it would open her up at other places too, not just on her neck. There aren't any marks showing she was dragged over rock. Or sand."

"But you said you suspected an animal?"

"The injuries looked like it. But now it crosses my mind somebody may have tried to cut her head off with something handy, something less sharp than a saw, but still sharp. Somebody might have interrupted him?"

"Fuck! You're obsessed with the old witch from Kampor, too."

"He wanted to cut her up to make sure she wasn't a demon. Maybe it's someone from town, someone really superstitious. When they were catching Andrei Chikatil, that guy who killed and ate fifty teenagers in Ukraine, they were helped by the fact that he was cutting their eyes out. At first they didn't know why, then they remembered the old belief that the image of the murderer shows in the eyes of his victim. That's why he massacred them. It led the investigation to someone superstitious."

Mungos was silent. Obviously I'd got his attention. But it was strange he hadn't thought of this before. He was only focused on the magician and his sexual delinquency. At one moment it even seemed he wanted to frame him for something, he was so obsessed by him. Just then the Motorola crackled.

He picked up and by the expression on his face I realized his working day had just started. They said something about the Match Girl and her things. The forensic team from Rijeka was searching her room.

"Let's go!" he said.

We were just at the heart clinic. We climbed up, went along the park toward the Imperial and then over the hotel parking lot down toward Palit. I couldn't help noticing the poster with the little poem about cutting was still in the window of the none too imperial bar. I thought about it as we walked down the road for Kampor toward the Aphrodita night club. But instead of turning toward the entrance into Stipe's club, Mungos kept walking. I could see the hole in the striptease entrepreneur's backyard was covered, but a mound was still visible. It looked like an unmarked grave.

The Match Girl had lived just behind the club in a typical, unfinished house made of concrete blocks with bare outside walls and no roof on the second level. There was also a small wooden shed with a pitched roof at one end of the first story. A staircase led to the imagined but unfinished parts. It seemed symbolic. In place of a garden gate, the two sections of the rosemary hedge were connected by yellow tape with the word police written across it. I watched Mungos shake hands with a very young man with an acne-scarred face, a memento of his pimpled youth. A police van, its trunk open, was parked in the uncultivated garden. I shook hands with the pimple face, which functioned something like a ticket to get us into the stuffy interior lit by spot lights.

Two men in protective gloves were taking prints. They pressed the foil against the furniture and larger, smooth-surfaced objects: windows, glasses, a cheap ceramic vase with a painting of the town and its four church towers. Pimple face, whose name—I'd just heard—was Goran and who was the chief inspector, gave Mungos a pair of protective gloves. I stood in the midst of the general search for something that, it seemed, stubbornly refused to be found. It was like some rare club of bug collectors, picking through their little universe with insane pedantry.

Mungos had introduced me as a pathologist and member of his team, so nobody paid any attention to me. I felt stupid just standing there so decided to look around, partly as a tourist, but also, I admit, out of professional curiosity. For pathologists the dead are a starting point, where the story begins. For others they're the end of the story, its result. I looked at the things in the room, the details of something whose consequences I'd had a chance to see in the wine cellar. The details were cheap and somewhat childish. The whole time I had the feeling we were searching through some child's room. A rubber figurine of a cricket with an umbrella, a derby hat, a long tailcoat. That was some cartoon character, for sure. The rubber on the cricket's right side was black and wrinkled. It looked like somebody had tortured it with fire. What would a Romanian hooker do with a rubber cricket? A toy? A memento? A sex prop? Then a brass fly the size of two closed fists. There was something oriental in the bend of its legs, reminding me of arabesques. It looked like a decorative figurine until one of the policemen lifted its wings and an empty space showed below. It turned into an ashtray. On the floor, next to the bed, there were several pairs of shoes and slippers, all lined up tidy. There was something horribly desperate in this tidiness. The slippers looked sad. I don't know why, but dead people's slippers have always moved me deeply. The shoes were different. Aggressive, with a very high heel, the kind that make legs stand straight. I love it when feet swoop down, when the skin on the ankles gets wrinkled and everything looks like a painful cramp. The pain makes the shoe more refined, adds the weight of the victim to the design. Japanese foot bending is only a little more radical. And the poor things whose high heels give them bloody blisters walk carefully all over the world, as if treading over little boys' balls. Had I seen her in those shoes, with that red hair and, of course, alive, maybe I too would have become one of the aspirants to her derriere.

An officer called the inspector, and Mungos joined them. I saw them examining some object, something of obvious interest because more officers from the island, who'd been indolently smoking outside, waddled up to see.

"Fero, come look!" Mungos said.

It was a rectangular box made of gilded metal, about five square inches in size. It was quite elegant. The inspector took it in his hand and weighed it. Then he opened it. The inside was covered with red muslin.

"A jewelry case!" I said.

But the inspector was suspicious. "Have a look!" he said, handing it to me. It almost fell out of my hands when I took it. It was extremely heavy. Everybody laughed.

"Have you ever seen such a heavy jewelry case?" he asked. He took it into his hands again and turned it. The gold back was similar to the front. There was a tiny white sticker in one corner, like a price tag but without any price, only some letters.

"What does it say?" Mungos asked. Several heads leaned in. We studied the inscription in small red letters. It was a small stamp of some kind. It said SECURITATE.

At first I didn't understand. Then one of the young police officers from the island asked what it meant.

"Romanian secret police," said the inspector.

I had a bad feeling about this.

9 A BACKYARD GRAVE

While Marijan, Mungos and I were fighting demons in the Kampor insane asylum, some comedian had spray painted yellow sex organs on the metal sculptures. Some had boy parts, some girl parts, and some both. The male organ was a stylized and unnaturally drawn out letter U, with two smaller Os on its top. The female was only an O divided in two parts with a vertical line. I saw this on my way home, walking toward the street recently renamed for the first Croatian king. The gray citizens seemed to have captured public interest again. But this time the interest was looser — a sneer had snuck its way in. The model citizens, angry with the genital painter, were gesticulating energetically because it was still unclear what it all meant. Because metal targets could always turn into national heroes, and vice versa. You had to treat them with dignity. Just in case and to be safe.

Near the top of Bobotina Street, in front of Bepa's house, was another such hero. I see Bepa working before her front door. She's brought out a little bottle of gas to the alley and is scrubbing the yellow johnson off the metal citizen with a little rag. And suddenly I realize both the first and the second, the drawing and the scrubbing, are a sign the islanders have accepted their gray neighbors. I watch Bepa scrub. She does it very gently, as if washing a real little boy's penis. I see she's developed a certain emotional attachment and is now publicly demonstrating it with this touching need for cleanliness. The spray painted dick the color of a lemon is very tough and doesn't give in easily to the gas and the rag. It looks like it won't give in to bleach either.

The smell of petroleum makes me realize what these metal citizens could be. But then again, it seems crazy.

Bepa says hi meanwhile and asks, "Have you seen, Fero? Dicks all over the place, like sardines."

I nod like somebody who understands. I actually do. It's a rare occasion for Bepa to deal with a male tool, even if it's only a drawing, and still stay clean, or pure, which is what she's been all her life, after all. Because cleaning's her job, her hobby, and, as far as I can see, her destiny. That's probably why I can't get rid of the tempting image: Bepa dusts the books down at the library, passes over the spines with her rug, opens one. You would think she's flipping through, interested in something, and then she suddenly closes the covers to kick the dust out. Then she pauses, glances left and right to see if anybody's watching, reaches inside and rips out a couple of pages at the end. Later maybe she'll use them for sanitation after visiting the toilet. But why she does it, God only knows. And maybe someone else on this island.

In front of my house there's a complete mess, the aftermath

of last night's storm. A loose shutter has knocked off some of the stucco. I bend down to remove it from the doormat and tap the mat gently against the wall to clean it. And keep me on its good side. Then I set it down nicely before the door just like my father did after his amputation. I still have both my legs, and I use them to wipe my feet with pleasure as I unlock the door.

I open it and notice a strange smell, something this house is not used to. The toilets stink, it's true, from the low pressure before the storm because the space wasn't aired. But the other smell, that's the strange one. Like somebody's been striking matches. Or lighting candles. It's interesting, and maybe dangerous, and it's why I open the windows in a panic, as if there could be a leak in a gas container that's been empty for ten years. I use the electric cooker. So now, as if it's time for spring cleaning, I open up my living space for the neighbors to see. Both the space and the mess. I'm a little ashamed because in the past few days I've created quite some chaos. I go into the kitchen and stack the dishes from the table in the sink. First I put in the pots, then the plates, vertically, and in the end I throw in the cutlery. And everything shines with the silver color of my father's stainless steel cookware with its lifelong warranty. In print.

Six years before I had to throw all our dishes away. Out of love. When my father was at the Stubičke Toplice rehabilitation center recovering from his amputation, I met my ex-wife. I used those three weeks, while my dad was learning to walk, to visit her in Zagreb. I was supposed to stay for three days, which was why I'd put all our dirty dishes, actually all the dishes we had, into the bathtub and tossed in a bottle of soap. As I was packing, the whole house smelled of lemon. But I stayed for three weeks, seven times longer, and when I got back, the stench from the bathroom was evident from the door. A green-ish mold that preserved in traces the aroma of the lemon scent-ed detergent lay across the water. And when I tried to pick up my "Good Morning" cup, the water would not let go. A long gooey line stretched from tub to cup. I couldn't break it. Like a slimy umbilical cord or a cobweb. Maybe I could have woven the web all through the house. I let the water drain and buried the dishes in the backyard. It looked like a small grave, like some alternative tomb for my mother in which a part of her metal dowry was interred. Then, before my father came home, I bought these stainless steel dishes on a loan. And they served him until he died.

But the smell of burning didn't go completely away even after the house had been aired out and the sharp Bura breeze had entered every room, even the pantry. Only then did it cross my mind that something might be fishy. As I was get-ting ready for bed, in a strange kind of daylight loneliness I remembered Marijan saying demons were always accompanied by an odor. And as I undressed, I noticed my watch was miss-ing. It was a silver diving Swatch my ex-wife had given me for our first anniversary. Together with that wind from the Velebit, I went back through every room of the house, but the watch was nowhere in sight. It had concealed itself somewhere like a pen. Or one of my old man's socks. Now it ticked away my time in secret.

Before going to sleep I had one more task, the one Mungos had left me. I called Franka and talked her into making Bobo invite us for dinner. It was easier than I thought. I fed her a story about hearing somewhere in town that said gentleman was just the man for prepping grilled mullets and he could grill the skin like no one else on the island. It'd be nice, I said, sweet-talking her, if I could heat up my own skin too. Of course, on the inside.

"It's a deal," Franka said, just the man for mullets.

Then, exhausted after a sleepless night and the demons from Kampor, I got into bed at last like one of those Swedes from a Bergman movie. Like the lead actor drawing dark curtains across the window to keep out the crisp polar daylight, I closed the blinds. But no dream came my way. Neither one of Bergman's nor any other. Probably because I was so tired. My thoughts ran to that grave for dishes in my backyard. Other people have hamsters, cats and dogs buried there. I have old pots. It's good I didn't set up a cross for them. May they rest in peace.

10 BALLET

Franka woke me with a phone call just as Mungos had a couple of days before. I had to get downstairs and pass before a large wall mirror. I was barefoot, wearing only my oversized boxers with little Snoopies all over them. Destiny probably wanted me to see them clearly. My ex-wife used to buy them for me. With love, but not without careful consideration. So I could see those cartoon characters—dogs, mice, squirrels—every day. She thought it would soften me up. By the end my dick had turned into a Snoopy.

Downstairs Franka spoke from the receiver: "Let's meet at Piazzetta in half an hour. Bobo bought the mullets."

"Okay," I replied. I wanted to add something, but she'd already hung up. It surprised me things had moved so fast.

At Piazzetta, she was sitting under the live oak. The Bura had cleared the air to an unimaginable transparency. In the distance, behind Frkanje, I could see Laganj and Dolfin Island, which were usually invisible because of the mist. On the right I made out the bluish contours of Lošinj. Franka was the only person on the square. She smiled when she saw me coming and got up so we could go.

The writer's aristocratic house was right around the corner. I couldn't help noticing the way Franka opened the wrought iron door that led to the garden. Routinely, as if she'd got used to it a long time ago. The garden, actually a small patio between the houses, was overgrown with vines and open to St. Euphemia Bay, and was filled with the smell of fish.

"The mullets," she said cheerfully as if she'd forgotten what was happening to her breasts. Baldie appeared at the kitchen door, carrying a kitchen towel in his hand. I paused for a moment, testing his reaction to my presence, and, realizing what was going on, he hurried to shake hands with me.

"Come in," he said. "Nothing to worry about."

For a moment I felt hurt.

"You can sit under the vines while Franka helps me with the potatoes!"

I confess he was master of the situation. He took Franka with him and left me a bottle of brandy. As consolation.

But it didn't take long before I had to admit the consolation wasn't at all bad. It was a very old walnut brandy that I didn't feel in my throat, like those instant ones, but in the top of my lungs, like Luka's best. Lately it seemed good drinks had somehow been finding me on their own. The clear weather gave the bay the green color of a lake, and a large boat with a bright green awning slid over the sea's dark green surface, probably carrying the last of the tourists from Frkanje to Škver. I'd seen postcards like this, immediately after my mother's death when we moved here to stay. I'd known the summer well from before. But in those years the fall unselfishly revealed itself me.

In addition to the banging of dishes, Franka's crackling laughter sometimes came from the kitchen. It was laughter that gave those it was meant for the impression that they were funny. Before the sad events with her breasts, she'd laughed loud and often. Now it all came back. At least for a moment. Then the silence fell again and in it I tried to make out what the two of them were doing there in the company of the parsley and potato salad.

Then, in one of those silent moments, I heard a third voice, very squeaky and frail. It was the voice of an old woman: "*Ma mi avete dimenticato?*"

It came from somewhere inside, like an aged, distorted echo of Franka's laughter. Some hypnotic old age that maybe wasn't destined for Franka. But Baldie had already, it seemed, left the kitchen and gone inside toward a room, and I could hear him say, "We had a nice potty, a bath, we put some cream on your tush. What else do you want now?"

Only then did I remember the bed-ridden old lady. And the memory quickly turned into the hope that Baldie had washed his hands before making dinner.

Before the food was ready for the table, Franka peeped out onto the patio, "You can come say hi to the old Miss!"

As I entered, a strong smell of urine came over me, the stench of uncontrolled excretions that was so common in old people's houses and that got into the walls, curtains, covers and carpets. I could still hear the squeaky Italian, like rubbing Styrofoam against glass, coming from the room: "*La restituzione ci sarà. Si si…* denationalization!"

"She's constantly raving about denationalization," said the

writer, standing next to the head of the old woman's bed, his arms crossed on his chest, as we entered the room. "Before she was raving about nationalization. It's terrible to think how she's been hoping all these years."

"Before the war she owned half the island," said Franka and then turned to the old lady. "Countess, how are you today?"

"Go fuck yourself, you and your countess," hissed the old lady as if speaking directly from her windpipe, skipping the vocal cords. "Stand there, you dead soul, and stop asking me nonsense!"

"She thinks she's talking to my late wife," Bobo explained.

I thought it must have been horrible for a middle-aged couple to look after this kind of primordial mummy, older than ichthyosaur itself, hoping every morning, every damn morning, the old woman would finally go to meet her maker, finally, thank the Lord, die and set them free to live what little was left of their lives in peace. Then suddenly the wife dies. As if the angel of death got confused and spit the blood clot into the wrong aorta.

We left them to talk, the old woman and Franka, dead woman to dead woman, and Bobo took on the task of showing me the house, meaning his study, which also served as his bedroom. It was the largest room in this aristocratic house. In the past it had been used as a salon. An unwieldy marital bed was crammed into it. The bedding lay scattered on one side while the other was covered with a green bedspread with grouses embroidered on it. Bookshelves lined all the walls like a spongy sound board in a radio booth. The books seemed to guard him from something. If he was hiding the video tape, I thought, it had to be here. Under the plane of his desk, also covered in books, I noticed several drawers and on one end a key inserted in the lock, most likely used to lock the drawers. And while the living example of my high school reading lists browsed through the rare manuals and antique medical books that might interest me as a doctor, I snooped around for the videotape. The room was obviously his asylum, a little empire protected from urinary fumes. Here he probably lived his solitary life. The only thing that surprised me was there was no TV or video player.

When we got back to the patio, Franka had already set the table and brought out the mullets and potato salad. At that moment Bobo placed several slices of bread on the still hot grill.

"I heard you're the man for mullets!" I said.

"Ah, yes, yes," he said, "but it's not the grilling. People are often mistaken about that. It's all about the feed. For example, lambs…"

"You're not going do it again, are you?" Franka said, smiling.

But he went on, ignoring her remark. "The lambs from Pag are so tasty because there even the grass is salty. They leap over those stones and eat aromatic herbs."

"Don't listen to him. Eat," Franka said.

I opened one of the mullets to take out its spine. It seemed well done with a nice, crunchy crust.

"And the mullets, excuse my French, feed on shit."

I raised my head for a moment, but then decided he wouldn't shake me. Or turn me off to the food. And this dinner was reminding me more and more of those meals from fables: the Fox invited the Stork…

"The turd is to them las bread is to us. The main food. And our countess does her number two every fortnight. She runs like clockwork. At least her shit is right on time in this town. And she stinks up the whole Gornja Street together with all the towers…"

144

"You don't have to be so graphic," said Franka, tucking into the head of one of the mullets.

I chewed on as well, but my teeth were dead.

"When she does her thing, I take her potty and splash it into the sea. Right here from this wall. Joy to the World! And St. Euphemia."

"He's lying!" said Franka. "He wants to impress you."

But the bald specimen of my high-school reading lists didn't seem like somebody who might be lying. Not now or when he fed that bread to the old ladies. I was beginning to see why he hated old age so much. Still he didn't look like someone who might be interested in girls with dicks. Or someone who, having fed the mullets, might go back to his room for a dose of well-hung entertainment.

"And you know what's best?" he said.

"No," I replied, continuing with my meal.

"Down here under the house is the best spot for mullets. On the whole island. And that's strange because there's no sand here..."

I saw through his game. He needed to have some fun in all this hell, and the circulation of turds in nature must have seemed like a good idea. That's why I decided to give him back his mullets. In his toilet. Just to complete one cycle. And for his other shit, that was between him and Mungos.

After the excellent dinner and three bottles of Vrbnička Žlahtina, which even made the squeaky old lady's voice sing, the writer hinted it was time for the old Miss' massage. He downed another glass, for courage, and went toward the room where the tiny old lady's hissing could be heard. Franka followed him. This shocked me. But after the first shock I realized it was my chance. So while they were dealing with the countess, I snuck into his study.

Through the half-open door, like in a film frame divided by a doorway and part of a wall, I could see Franka and the writer massaging the old lady. Franka opened the sheets while he was still going on about denationalization. Under her shirt the old lady was completely naked. Two bony legs were stuck out of her barrel-like body, swollen with fluid. In the meantime I rummaged through the writer's private paradise. I began with the desk. The top drawer contained office thingies: two packs of paper clips, a stapler, an old blotter from when people still used quills. There was a lot of paper for a typewriter, but I didn't see one anywhere. In the second drawer there were bills, notebooks, old photographs. But the tape wasn't there. It was good the door was slightly open so I could see what Franka and the writer were doing in the other room.

They were more than busy. Baldie gently took the old woman by her upper body and, explaining the basics of restitution, turned her on her side. She had no behind. Actually, there were only bones from which the wrinkled skin hung loose. It looked as if the muscles had disappeared. On her thighs there were decubitus ulcer wounds. Meanwhile, Franka took a bottle of something, probably alcohol, and a little gauze, and, while the bald headed writer held the old woman on her side with his hand, she began gently massaging what was left of her buttocks. The old creature huddled in a fetal position as if she were about to be born again.

Just as I decided to search the bookshelf opposite the door, my attention was drawn to one of the books on the desk, an old edition of *Master and Margarita*. Other books were more recent. I don't know what made me check it. But as I opened it, shock.

Meanwhile, Franka and Baldie were busy with the old lady. Their movements reminded me of ballet. They were perfectly in sync, their flow natural. The massage flowed from the raising of the shirt, the raising of the shirt from the turning of the body. There was no waste of energy, just composed concentration. And everything happened in silence. Franka smiled. It was their game. When everything was over, the writer lowered the old lady's long shirt with his free hand, as if drawing the curtain on a puppet theater.

One moment I watched him and a second later my eyes turned to the inside of the book. Actually there was no inside. A large hole, the size of a yogurt cup, gaped at me. The pages had been cut out, creating an empty space in the shape of a circle. There was an inscription in red capital letters (obviously done on a children's printing press) on the front page: "This book's meaning has deepened." I opened other books on the desk. They were hollow too, with the same inscription. I was slowly putting the pieces together. A writer. High literature, small print runs, and the islanders read only thrillers. Who wouldn't hate them? Especially if he could turn everything into some kind of a project, a kind of avant-garde. It turned out I actually went through the same thing everybody goes through when they're searching for something: Looking for a video tape, I turned up the person who'd been defacing the novels. Right before Franka's nose. Next to the books, on the desk, there was a small printing press for children.

Then I saw the cardboard box under one of the shelves. It threw me to my knees because I had to take it out first. And as I was removing the dusty box on all fours like a police dog, two feet in light pants appeared in front of my nose.

"Can I help you?" said the feet in a voice unmistakably like the writer's. There was no surprise in his tone. Only irony.

I got up and turned red at the same time. As if he'd caught me on top of a six-year old girl.

"Interesting room," I said. Best I could do. In the other room Franka was saying something to the old woman, who laughed. I didn't remember her laughing once during the evening. I cleaned the nonexistent dust from my knees and stood by the opinion that in situations like this, any movement was helpful. Meanwhile, after he'd looked me up and down long enough, the writer went to one of the shelves and reached behind the books, though first glancing at Franka to see where she was. Then he took out the tape, an ordinary tape in a cardboard cover with worn out flaps. Probably from frequent use.

"Is this what you're looking for?"

I began apologizing, mumbled something about forgiveness and stuff, but he remained completely cold.

"Go ahead and take it to Hrvoje. I haven't watched it."

I can't say I wasn't curious why the writer had got hold of the tape if he didn't have either a video player or a TV. But at that moment, standing in front of him with the fluff balls of his carpet on my knees and knowing the terrible truth that he was the one destroying the endings of novels, I was too ashamed to ask. I dialed Mungos' number and, worried that Franka might see me with the tape, carefully snuck out.

Mungos got to the main square in record time. He must have been close by. He snatched the tape as if it were of vital importance. I had the impression he'd met me here so I wouldn't have a chance to see which of our fellow citizens played the lead. He pinched my cheek and said, "Well done, Fero!"

When I got back, Franka was saying something about Latin sails. About the fact that they best fit the winds of this region and people of old weren't stupid. The writer stood by the sink, carefully drying the old cobalt set plates that most likely belonged to the bed-ridden Miss. It was one of the gentlest contacts between a man and a dish I'd ever seen. It allowed him not to pay attention to me. The awkwardness was interrupted by the sound of the island's brass band making its way from the Loggia toward St. Christopher's Square. It told us the fiesta had begun.

I I FIESTA

The band was making a lot of noise. Franka hopped over the slippery stone slabs, hurrying down toward the Loggia, as if she might miss part of those early-autumn festivities. Her haste was touching. I walked behind, and again it crossed my mind in the midst of the brass and the potpourri of parlor ballads I should tell her I loved her. That I'd loved her maybe all this time, since Renata had grown so insolently. That her not socializing with men came as a magnificent caprice to me. I could tell her this now. But she wouldn't take me seriously, thank God. It was probably more that she came to my mind every time I felt lonely. Even now, when my manhood was still recovering from cartoons. And so, without any awkward words, we got to Srednja Street right amid the procession crawling behind the band. This urge to express my feelings every time there was a lot of noise seemed familiar, as if I'd seen it somewhere and then completely forgotten where.

After a while I could see only Franka's head. She was hopping among other town heads whose faces I didn't know anymore. We all came together at St. Christopher's Square, which was decorated with flags and balloons. On its western end they'd set up a stage with a stand and mic for speakers. I noticed the metal citizen standing by the pharmacy was now pushed all the way to the wall, out of people's way. Then the music broke off and a short blond man with a long blond moustache that fell over his lips in the shape of an upside down U climbed on stage.

"The Mayor!" said Franka, appearing next to me again.

And he began: "Ladies and gentlemen, fellow citizens... We stand amid difficult times weighted with problems and misfortunes, and the worst misfortune of all is this war that fell upon us there from the Velebit. But, my dear fellow citizens, even in these difficult times we need to continue leading a normal life... which is why this year we welcome as well our friends from other European countries."

He made an emotional pause, allowing us to think a little about our friends from other European countries, especially about what countries they came from and how weighty they were. A giggle made its way through the crowd. Somebody had remembered the fat tourists from the slimming program at the Hotel Imperial.

He went on: "We welcome our dear friends as well as we can. Under the given circumstances. But we've also encountered some new ones..."

Just then two young men wearing medieval archers' uniforms brought one of those metal heroes to the stage. The town went silent. St. Christopher's Square, packed with people, was tense with silence. It seemed the birds and the boats fell silent too. And maybe the squirrels. The speaker, satisfied with this tense silence, went on cheerfully: "All of you must have been asking yourselves who are these noble people who have shown up on our streets. My dear fellow citizens, they are metal gentlemen from our sister town of Telgte. I don't even have to mention that in these difficult times we've made many friends all across Europe. Among them are the people of the historic town of Telgte in the north of Germany. At the beginning of this month they provided us with priceless humanitarian aid, and now is the moment that, together with the mayor of the heroic town of Telgte, I announce happy news to you…"

A tall, handsome man in his fifties, with Prussian posture and a tidy moustache, in a dark blue blazer with silver buttons, climbed on stage. The two mustachioed mayors broke bread together and began chewing it, carefully and ceremoniously as if they were dining on the body of Christ. And after he'd swallowed, the mayor with the longer moustache went on, "I hereby pronounce Telgte our sister city!"

For a moment everybody was dead silent. Then a couple of people began to clap. The applause soon spread like the flu, even among those who, like Franka and me, had never before heard of the town of Telgte.

"They gave us money for the road and the new boardwalk," someone behind me said.

"And what's with the statues?" I whispered in Franka's direction. She shrugged.

The mayor was still addressing the island masses. This was obviously a moment of unforgettable triumph for him because he'd managed to keep the secret for two whole days.

"This is why we started a joint project under the title *The Shadows of Speed Surround Us Everywhere*. It is a traffic project envisioned by mayor Grünwald…."

The mustachioed Prussian in the blue blazer bowed at the mention of his name. All of us looked at him in amazement. At that moment it dawned on me that Bepa had washed the penis of her metal hero out of intuition. It was in front of her house that they'd placed it. I remembered the old man from Vela Riva who'd said that one of them was at Frkanje. That was most likely for Igor.

"And that's why we are raising these symbolic monuments

for our dear fellow citizens who were taken too early from our lives because of speed...."

I wanted to glance at my watch. The encounter with an empty wrist was very discomforting, as if the missing object was trying to tell me something. The mayor concluded, "The dead are among us!"

Several speakers followed the mayors, and it all ended up with the ox on the spit that had been spinning like a promise behind stage. Here words have, from time immemorial, been just an introduction to gluttony. But in this half hour a lot was said. Mostly about the metal citizens and the heroic town of Telgte, whose project had reduced the number of traffic deaths in their town and its surrounding area to a minimum. Because when a driver sees a gray citizen next to the road, he automatically slows down. He thinks, I don't want to be like you and get scorched by the sun and let crows shit all over me. The only problem was that on the island there were no fast roads where they could put up the metal warnings. So our authorities had erected them like tombstones next to the houses of those who'd been killed. Or at the scene of an accident. I thought the families whose dear ones had lost their lives now had to be feeling awful. And so did whoever had been drawing the penises, though, when you think about it, he wasn't incorrect....

"Even if they give us their money, we don't have to accept their nonsense!" Franka whispered.

"I think we have to," I said. I was convinced of it. "Then we'll get more humanitarian aid. Now that tourism's gone, we have to look in other directions."

"Yuck," blurted Franka.

She stood in front of me and I placed my hands on her shoulders. She took it well. I was pretending to be listening to the members of the town government, but in fact I was thinking about the ballet with the old countess. Why did it bother me so much now? And would I have the courage to tell her who'd been destroying the books? This was exactly what I was thinking about, the books, when a whisper spread through the crowd, a commotion. Even the speaker paused. Those fixing the ox raised their heads too. We stood like that for a while, in silence again, not knowing what was going on. Then the policeman got onto the stage and whispered something into the speaker's ear, who passed on the message in a whisper to the mayor, who was still standing on stage. But our mayor said nothing to the German one. Then the policeman said my name into the mic, politely asking me to come to the police station.

12 NOTHING BUT BREAKING GLASS

The crime team from Rijeka was getting into a police speedboat at the small pier near the station. A man with two German shepherds was standing on shore. The dogs were sitting, breathing hard.

Mungos came toward me. "They've found her," he said.

He was shaken and for the first time didn't know what to do with himself. He looked completely useless. I didn't know what had shocked him so much, that they'd found Mirna's body or what he'd seen on the tape. If he'd had enough time to see it. We got on board. I shook hands with Goran and the other members of the team. Meanwhile, Mungos helped them load their gear. I saw two metal cases with tools and the official photographer, who was chewing something that looked like carob root. We were a very quiet team.

"The dogs found her half an hour ago," Mungos said. But nobody responded. It seemed each of us was immersed in his own thoughts, as if concentrating on the encounter with the dead girl. I started feeling somewhat weak and found I couldn't breathe all that well. The pain in my chest grew stronger as we were about to leave the port. It wasn't good.

"Do you remember that guy from the funeral who was with me all the time?" I asked Mungos suddenly. He looked at me as if this was the first time he'd seen my face.

"No," he replied. "Why is that important?"

"Just asking," I said. "No one remembers him and he seemed local. Shorter guy, little goatee. Knows everybody on the island."

"I don't know," he said and was probably thinking, leave me alone.

The boat briefly raised its beak at full speed and then began to slow. I saw we were going toward the small pier on the Island of St. Juraj, which stood across from the harbor. In our youth, we used to swim to the island and had our birthday parties there. One of the policemen went to the bow and waited to tell to the driver when to reverse engine. Then he jumped out and tied the rope around the column. The other one threw out the anchor. While the policemen were taking out the gear, Mungos led me and Goran up. We walked over the thick, thorny cover of pine needles. The smell of pines mixed with that of iodine and out there behind Frkanje the sun was just setting. They'd picked the best time to find the dead little girl.

We found her on shore, somewhere at the island's middle point, in a sitting position, facing the open sea. Her back leaned against the trunk of a pine. Her little dress, once white, now had large red spots of dirt all over it. Down below, at the bottom, where her legs were, laced flounces protruded from under it. Her arms lay peacefully against her body while two pine branches supported her under the armpits, probably so the body wouldn't slide down. She was facing Italy. If there are dreams in death, I thought, she must be dreaming about stores. It was sale season. Little sneakers, gym shoes, a school bag with cat's eyes and Snoopy on it. She would have been starting school in fall.

"She doesn't stink as much as you would expect," said Goran. This was a surprise. The smell of the decomposing body was not intense, as if something had prevented the rotting process. Perhaps it was the wind? The salt? Mungos brought the hand-kerchief to his nose and bent down to have a better look. I did the same. Somebody handed me a pair of gloves.

"She doesn't seem to have been raped," I said after a while. Only then did I notice she was sitting on a large, pink beach towel. The pine needles had covered it in the meantime. Toys were scattered all around the body, probably the ones Renata had put in her coffin.

The team came with their gear. One of the policemen began marking the area with a yellow line, the word police written on it. He was tying it around the pines. Others had already begun examining the terrain. Mungos squatted next to the body, his eyes looking toward Italy. He was thinking.

"What won't a man do to get his disability pension?!"

"You think?" I said. "Or he's just really crazy?"

We found a thermos with mint tea in it and a plastic cup. The policemen were looking for prints. We laid the body out carefully so I could do the necessary examination. One of the policemen was gathering the toys, probably looking for something suitable for taking prints. I didn't miss the rubber figu-rine of a cricket. This one wore a red dress with white spots and a handbag. It was the wife of the charred cricket we'd found in the Little Match Girl's room. I told Mungos to take it. It wasn't any good for prints.

Meanwhile, even without a thorough examination I could confirm that the body had not been sexually abused. The toys, after all, indicated a different motive.

"Any suspects?" Goran said, addressing Mungos.

"There's a guy who keeps on talking about her. He can't get her off his mind. He says the friars raped her in her coffin."

Mungos would have liked it if Ranko had dug her out. But we were abandoning that idea.

"Do you remember that woman? Krstinić," I said. "She said the girl was under the stars. And she was on the island. Well this is the island on the island. Why would somebody hide the body on this island?"

Mungos thought for a moment and said, "So the dogs couldn't find it."

"What else did she say? What was the demon like?"

"Sad," Mungos answered. And then the thing slowly penetrated his mind. You could tell by his face. It seemed as if his facial features somehow jumbled and then came back to their places, like cards. Now they showed something between horror and compassion.

"How could she know?" he managed to squeeze out. But that wasn't important anymore. He came up to Goran, who gave short instructions to the policemen with the prints. There were several rather well preserved prints on the foil. Enough to identify somebody.

Two uniformed policemen from the island carried the little body. It was wrapped in the pink beach towel from which the pine needles kept falling. There was no more need to examine it. An autopsy under these circumstances was out of the question. We knew the cause of death. We followed in silence, as if at a small funeral. And from town the wind carried pieces of those brass band arias I knew so well from sitting on the island's terraces: *Oprosti mi pape, Nadalina, Tornerò*.

We watched as they carefully loaded the body into the rocking speedboat. Two members of the team followed them. Mungos was saying something into his Motorola. I realized he was talking to the doctor from the office in town. As the boat pulled out, the three of us sat on the steps under the lighthouse and listened to the music from town. We sat like that for a while, in silence. I saw the ambulance turning toward town and the police station on its way to meet the boat. I thought about how in my irrational fear of having children some unidentified image of a speedboat carrying a child's body played an important role. And how somehow this had eaten up the love between me and my wife.

I don't know how much time passed before Mungos' Motorola crackled again. He handed it to Goran, and from the inspector's face, as he listened, I realized he knew who needed to be arrested. Supposedly, they'd found the boat used to transport the body on Škver.

"Come with us," Mungos told me while Goran was still on the phone.

"Why?" I asked, but really I should have said I didn't feel like it, I had no business there, it was police business.

"To make it easier for me," he said. The policeman in him suddenly became a friend.

And so, driving in Mungos' Land Rover through the deserted streets — most of the people were still at the fiesta — we reached Globus' house on Palit. We found them, all three of them, under the vines. The tablecloth had changed in the meantime. It wasn't the one with fruit anymore. Globus and his mother were slurping their soup. It smelled of cooked chicken.

Renata was lying in a deck chair next to the table. Now she seemed shorter, or at any rate that height of hers wasn't so visible in this position. She was completely oblivious. Globus got up from the table and shook our hands in silence. In the past few days his beard and hair had grown a little, like brand new moss just out of the ground. It seemed he'd been expecting us. Even so, Mungos took him into the kitchen while the old woman offered the two of us chairs and asked if we wanted some soup. Renata didn't react. We sat in silence.

The sound of breaking glass came from the kitchen. There were no other sounds, neither yelling, nor swearing, nor crying. Only the glass. Right then God decided to have some fun with the old lady's bowels. She farted so loud you could have heard it from the center of town. Goran and I pretended nothing had happened, she hadn't farted. It somehow hovered between us while Globus was in the kitchen settling accounts with his glasses and plates. It took some time.

When he finally appeared at the door, all covered in tears, we knew the first wave of horror had passed and now things might be easier. Goran approached the deck chair but Renata had already got up. She walked very uncertainly. We supported her under her arms.

"Where, in the name of God, are you taking her?" the old lady hissed.

Mungos hugged her and said now we had to take her to Kampor, but we'd bring her back home once she was better.

"I just wanted to see if her fingernails had grown!" Renata said. "I know what I've done."

So we took her to the car while Globus followed, carrying her toiletry case. The old lady remained standing under the vines and watched us, her eyes etched in my memory.

I was still thinking about them when, a couple of hours

later, Mungos and I climbed up to the cemetery. Things were already back in place. The police tape had been removed, the grave was covered. It all seemed peaceful and normal. As if Mirna had gone back home. The only witnesses to the tragedy were the side paths dirty with red dust. Even the hopscotch had disappeared. As we were walking back down one of those paths, I saw a ribbed footprint of a man's shoe and next to it a mark of a dog's paw in the concrete. At first the tracks seemed idyllic, friendship between man and dog hardened in concrete. Then I thought about it. In all my forty some years, I'd never once seen a dog and its master at the cemetery. I'd seen stray dogs, for sure, but a man and his dog never. It didn't belong here — a dog running around, marking the terrain and peeing over the places of final repose. Besides, there was just a single footprint of a man next to single one of a dog. It was bizarre, as if the person had one dog's leg. Just then I felt the pain in my chest again and couldn't breathe. I heard Mungos screaming, "What's wrong? What's wrong?"

Then I must have collapsed.

St. Clare's Rain

I called in that I wouldn't be coming to work for a while. Except perhaps as pathological material.

From my hospital bed I watch the terrace Renata and I used to come to back then, in those happy days when a heart was still good for love and a penis for pleasure. Not like today: my heart's fit only for a cardiogram, my penis for a catheter. I'm confined by wires leading from my body to machines, rooted in technology, slowly turning into a robot, steel, bakelite, copper tubing. A man of the future. My breathing sounds like a goat passing gas, which I'm sure can be heard through the open window.

I'm being treated by Doctor Feri Bernstein, a classmate of mine from the university. In the intervening years, he specialized in hearts, and I in dead people. Probably because he was afraid of the dead. I was afraid of the living. I didn't know he was on the island.

We met in an interesting position: me lying on a stretcher, barely alive and in a state of semi-consciousness, him standing above me with a stethoscope. We formed a cross. Horizontal and vertical distinguished colleagues. This would be God's signature if he were illiterate. When I saw him, I thought I was about to leave for good and my old friends were visiting me in my hallucinations. Feri Bernstein was a Hungarian Jew from

Subotica who'd moved to Opatija with his parents when he was ten. His full name was Ferenc, an unusual name in Opatija so they'd screwed around with him at school. That's how he became Feri. We had similar nicknames.

It was a fresh fall evening. While I wheezed through my slime-filled lungs, a life-saving oxygen-filled breeze streamed in through the window.

That friend of mine between my legs began waking up unexpectedly and with the catheter it was very uncomfortable. Painful. I was probably aroused by some shadow from my subconscious. Or from the terrace nearby. Anyhow, after this awakening, the electrodes and machines responded with a sound that was far worse than any alarm clock. A nurse, whose greatest virtue was her compactness, flew into the room, swift and wiry. She injected something into my vein to calm the excessive activity of my heart and most likely make me urinate without control. Then she added, "You have a visitor!"

At this time of night?

Just then Feri Bernstein's bald head appears at the door. Franka comes in just behind with an unnatural smile on her face, as if she's got a staple in her mouth. She sits down on a round chair next to my bed—the nurse usually sits there when she's working on my lower gear—while Feri stands over my temperature chart. This is probably his professional position. From there he can look at the face of his patient and the graph at the front of the bed at the same time. Then he ponders whether they're in agreement.

"You're okay!" says Feri professionally. To calm me down. "We put you on machines to control your heart activity."

Franka says, "I cleaned up your house. I threw away everything that had gone bad!"

That's Franka. At hell's doorway she worries about rotten potatoes. Things like this allow her to stay on Earth.

"Tomorrow we'll take him off the machines," says Feri. "Then you can bring him something to eat. I'm on call tonight so I'll see you later. I'll leave you for now…"

His discrete retreat puts Franka in an awkward position. I'm up to my neck in it, covered with a bed-sheet because down there I'm completely naked with a catheter. It wouldn't be nice if Franka saw me all tied up and wrinkly there for the first time after twenty years of friendship.

"You've been here for two days," she says. "Yesterday they didn't let me see you because you were asleep. Mungos called me so I took your things home."

This conversation is going nowhere. I don't know what to ask her.

"What's going on outside?" I say. Best I can do.

"There's a truce up there so more police came. They took over all three floors of the station. They're bringing people in for questioning. Where they were, what they saw, things like that. Serious business."

"And Renata?"

"Somebody told me, I think Tomo, that her condition's being evaluated at Kampor. She won't be indicted."

Then we stop, as if observing a moment of silence. She puts orange juice on my nightstand, probably so I have enough material to pee out through that little tube. Then she cleans the trash from the top of the cabinet — paper, pieces of nylon, something they took off an iv bottle.

"There's more," she says after a bit. "They've found the children!"

The machine almost started screaming again. Anyhow, I felt some activity in connection with either my blood pressure or my heart.

"And you know how? The story about the children spread around the island, people said they appeared at night. Marija Pende, my godmother, saw her kid's bed—she has a seven year old son—it was full of wet sand. She realized he'd been going out at night. Other children went with Stipe's daughter, to look for the Schnauzer."

"Fucking dog nocturne! But why at night?"

"A joke, an adventure, I don't know. Anyhow, the children thought it was more interesting at night. And somebody spread the word the dog had been resurrected and it was showing up after midnight."

Then, it seems, I was overcome by weakness again because the resurrected Schnauzer and my father's missing socks some-how got mixed up in my head. Soon Franka said goodbye. I don't even remember what she said as she left. But I told her to bring me something to read. I'd probably slept for a couple of hours because, when Feri's hand on my face woke me up, the usual sounds of the hospital had gone. And I couldn't hear anything happening outside.

"How are you?" he asked.

Considering he'd woken me up in the middle of the night and I was plugged into machines, it wasn't a very appropriate question. But Feri seemed bored and anyhow I'd had enough sleep in the past two days. I tried to sit up, and he immediately removed the electrodes. This was strange.

"The results are back," he said. "You don't need this."

"What's wrong with me?" I asked because Feri was obvious-ly in the mood for conversation and this meant for a diagnosis as well. "Did I almost... take the trip?" I asked.

"Not exactly. Actually, it depends. You never know with these things."

"What things?"

"Well, with trips," he said. "For example, I've taken quite a few."

And then he began telling me a story about Venice and the first time he served on a passenger ship as a doctor. I could tell he was beating around the bush. Something didn't allow him to be direct. It was easier for him this way. Not all doctors were like Leichenbegleiter, who looked at the doormat before his door as he delivered his diagnosis. Some were uncomfortable. And I'd actually never heard this story about his first sea voyage. I only knew that every summer he'd sail on huge passenger liners taking care of the hearts of German retirees. The boat he'd embarked on in Venice was doing a cruise around the eastern Mediterranean. Feri got close with some Otto, a Volksdeutscher from somewhere near Subotica. Otto was the same age as Feri and was traveling with his aging father. After WWII they'd escaped from Yugoslavia, and the whole family had lived in Münster ever since. Their homeland brought them together even though Feri was a Jew and a good part of his family disappeared in German concentration camps. Otto's father Franz was sickly, so Feri often took his blood pressure and gave him medications. The old man had a hard time dealing with the weather, which grew hotter as they moved south.

When they came to Israel and docked in Haifa, the old gentleman, who'd spent his life working as a hotel receptionist in Germany, and later as a tourist agent in Yugoslavia, didn't want to set foot on Israeli soil. His son and Feri tried to talk him into going, but in vain. The old man remained firm. That evening Feri went out with the passengers. The German tourists went through the border control without any problems, probably because of their convertible Deutsch Marks, but he was held back. A police officer studied his passport. Then they ordered him to take his clothes off. There was a dog there as well. Strangely, he was most embarrassed by the dog. Four men, two policemen and two Israeli soldiers with machine-guns, stood there completely indifferent to his nakedness. He covered his private parts with his hand. The dog was the only one looking at him. It was a German shepherd. He stood there completely naked in front of the four armed men with helmets and a German shepherd. One of the policemen put on a rubber glove in order to examine the reachable parts of his insides. In the end, when everything was over, a police captain asked him ironically, returning his passport, "Why does Yugoslavia not have diplomatic relations with Israel?"

Later on, on the Hotel Medina terrace, as he sipped his lemonade, he thought about that biggest humiliation of his life. He knew he should never tell his father at home. Or if he did he'd have to leave out a lot. The German tourists danced to the sounds of Hava Nagila. They were having a lot of fun. He sat there in case somebody broke their leg or hurt themselves in any old way. It's what he was being paid for. He thought about all that, felt sick, and stormed into the toilet to vomit everything there was to vomit. But as he came out of the stall to wash his mouth, he noticed an older woman with European features taking money for the toilet service. On their way out of the bathroom, the tourists would drop coins into her plate. She'd then say something that sounded like thank you in a language that sounded something like German.

A guide told him later this was Frau Schlezinger, a German Jew who had miraculously survived Buchenwald. God's ways, like all his decisions, are always hard to understand. God had saved Frau Schlezinger from a concentration camp so now, in her free homeland, she could charge Germans for peeing.

When he went to vomit for the second time, the woman was singing.

He returned to the ship very late, and old Herr Franz had gotten sick. He'd gone pale and kept opening his mouth as if he was chewing large chunks of air. His pulse was weak. Something had to be done soon. They carried him into the ship's emergency room, laid him down, and gave him a strong medication for urination. Feri remained with him and held his hand. After a while, the old man perked up. He looked at him with watery eyes.

"You know why I didn't go out?" his voice crackled. "At the end of the war I was mobilized by the s.s. units in Novi Sad. We had very tough training, even maneuvers with live ammunition. In the end, each of us got a machinegun. They would bring several very skinny Jews before us to shoot them. This was the final exam. I watched their faces as I fired my gun. One of them had margarine around his mouth. They had given them food before they brought them in front of the firing squad. They knew this way they would be calm."

The old man explained that now, when he was slowly becoming senile, this was the thing he could not forget. The margarine. That and the image from his childhood in Subotica: a red-hot metal sheet the Gypsies had used to train baby bears to dance.

"Do you know what it was?" Feri said. He wasn't expecting an answer from me, but nor was he avoiding his anymore. "Angina Pectoris! The old man would never have told me those things if he wasn't sure he was about to die. That's what it seems like. Angina Pectoris feels like Judgment Day, but you live with it. True, it's like living with a nasty old woman, but you still live with it. You'll be all right. We've given you some medication."

About an hour after the fourth noon Franka brought me lunch, a nice veal soup with homemade gnocchi. They'd taken me off the machines, removed the catheter, and moved me into a regular room, so I was finally able to eat like a human being. As I was slurping the salt-free stew—a real hospital treat—she entertained me with the news.

"I found your watch," she said. "You left it in your sink, with the dishes. At first I didn't notice it because it's the same color as those forks you have."

This was something new. Nothing like that had happened to me before, as if something had taken control. Then she took out the books and put them on the bed to make some room on the nightstand. She removed the tea cup, a pack of juice, and the plastic container for my medications and put everything in the corner of the little night table. Then she took the books from the bed and put them there as well. There were quite a few.

"What have you brought?" I asked between two spoonfuls. The soup was quite tasty.

"Some are from your house. I found this one on your night-stand, beside your bed."

It was an old book. I knew its title from somewhere. Axel Munthe's *The Story of San Michele*. But I hadn't been reading much since I got here. And before that, I hadn't been here for at least five years, ever since my father's death. So somebody else must have been reading this thing, probably my father, and now Franka had brought it to me to finish. A nice little misunderstanding. There were also George Mikes' *How to be an Alien*, Vitomil Zupan's *Leviathan*, and a couple of titles by Raymond

Chandler. For my free time. Obviously, she'd taken these from the library.

"Have they got their endings?" I asked.

She smiled. "If they don't, I'll tell you how they end." She was in a good mood. I thought it was because she had a comrade in illness now. Things were falling into place, as if we were becoming a sect. So I felt now was a good moment.

"Your friend, Bobo…" I said.

"What about him?"

"He's the one destroying the books. I figured it out the day before yesterday, when we were at his place. I found some on his desk. Their middles were hollow. And there was an inscription: 'This book's meaning has been deepened.' Probably some project of his. Avant-garde. You can tell by his face he doesn't like popular literature. People like him hate bestsellers."

Franka watched me with an expression of pity on her face. Not because I was sick, but because of the books. And the bald writer, most likely. Still, I got her thinking about all these things, though they were irrelevant here. She followed some thought of hers as she tidied the inside of my hospital nightstand and threw out some old magazines that had obviously belonged to a previous patient. And then she washed her hands in the washstand, smiled into the mirror, and checked her front teeth.

"I'm sure it's not Bobo," she said in a serious voice after she'd finally looked away from her upper crowns. "But I'm thinking something else. For a while that friend of yours was hanging around with Bobo. He told him he was interested in literature. He got all whiny because he hadn't studied comparative literature in Zagreb. He even helped him with the countess."

168

"Maskarin?" I said. This was news. I couldn't imagine him in such a role.

"Now I see," she said. "That's how he got the idea. His godfather from Rijeka is a book sales rep. He'd already offered us all kinds of books through this godfather of his, but we didn't get any because we were well stocked. The city still has some money left."

"And crime novels are what people read most," I said. "They read only after the tourists are gone."

Franka was now hooked on the idea. "Think about it. Destroying a crime novel is the easiest way. Then you just need to accuse some unknown madman for it. We've got enough nuts around. Kampor is full of them. That's his calculation. If he destroys the reserve of the most widely read things, the city will have to go through that godfather of his... Understand?"

I understood all too well, like alimony and expensive slippers. Maskarin's masks were actually very obvious, and the only image in which I could now see his face was him picking at what had been left of Franka's sea bass.

After lunch I slept for a while and then on my own two feet limped into the toilet to pee. I felt so proud, even though my thing was still burning from the catheter. The matches had got into my urine too though, luckily, for a different reason. I set my pillows, made myself comfortable in bed, and reached for the book by Axel Munthe. Beneath the title there was an inscription: *Confessions of a Blind Author*. This was my mother's favorite book. It was about an ambitious Swedish doctor who got himself a job in Paris where he treated rich patients. The book recounted the doctor's adventures. Really appropriate for a hospital. One summer, on his journey, the doctor fell in love with the Island of Capri and the ruins of Tiberius' villa, which offered a magnificent view of the sea. He bought a piece of the complex and spent the rest of his life investing every dime into the reconstruction of the villa. He'd been earning good money as a doctor in Paris. But when he'd finally restored the house, the gardens, pillars and colonnades, he was overcome by blindness. It was the kind of hero my mother liked.

As I flipped through the book, I landed on a chapter entitled "The Corpse Chaperon," which was somehow too familiar, and to my horror stumbled upon the word "Leichenbegleiter." This was a hunchback who accompanied the deceased in their coffins in German trains around Lübeck. How could that supposed friend of mine from the funeral know the word I'd seen and forgotten so long ago? He'd returned it to me by inventing the story about the doormat inside the office door. But what if he hadn't invented it? I felt terror spreading gradually from somewhere in my abdomen. I flipped through the book in a panic and then somewhere near the end found the life-saving stamp of the island library. The list in the back, where the due dates were usually put, had been ripped out. There were traces of glue on the back cover, but the stamp was enough evidence that for a while the adventures of the Swedish doctor were available to the whole population of the island. This calmed me somewhat, but still I tossed away the book, which had two stylized boats on the cover as if it had been listed on the Vatican's index of banned titles.

Nervous and uneasy, I turned to the American crime novels until the evening, when Marijan came. The friar showed up at the door just as some guy from the novel had decided to use a shard of glass to disfigure the face of the woman who'd betrayed him. He said he had walked over from the monastery and he understood why I hadn't called.

"So? Are you here as a friend or as a priest?" I chirped from bed. I was happy to see him.

"It's up to you," he said, taking the nurse's chair for washing one's lower parts. He gathered his habit like women gather their skirts to sit, and put his hand on my forearm. "You know, Fero, you haven't deserved this!"

"Friar Marijan, it can't be you're still mad at me," I whined, certain he'd forgiven me that toilet indiscretion.

"Tell me! How did it all happen? I'll give you your last rites later."

"I felt it first in the police boat as we were going to Školjić. Pressure in my chest. I didn't want to see Mirna out of her grave... you know. Later everything was fine. Both on the island and at Renata's house. It really caught up with me at the cemetery, when I saw..."

"Yes, it gets to you!" Friar Marijan mumbled into his beard. "The cemetery's a likely spot."

"I mean, I wasn't that upset then. Still, I saw a footprint in the concrete, a man's shoe, with a ribbed sole, and one dog's, how should I put it, foot."

"So?"

"It seemed like it was a man with a dog's leg. He walks around the cemetery."

"And what are you trying to say?" Marijan got a little upset and his face grew strict.

"Nothing. Just these coincidences... they got on my nerves a little."

"Guilty conscience. That's what it is," he said. "You've already got your doctor's diagnosis. And now you want the other one from me, eh? He saw a footprint and he got upset. All kinds of shit have piled up in your veins a long time ago. In your veins and your soul, if you still have one. So now you think that was the same gentleman we saw in Kampor. Let me tell you. It's not that the devil doesn't exist. But he doesn't just show up like that... You're sick, but you aren't stupid. You really surprise me. And you know I always liked you most when you were in the choir and at church. And the fact that you were coming to your Sunday school in secret..."

"And how should he show up..." I started kidding with the friar. "As, let's say, the president of the city council?"

"How's your tool?" God's servant spat out the word. Now he was quite upset. "The thing is you always recognize him when he arrives. And that's individual. And all those things, the smell of sulfur, goats' feet... that's all nothing. Throw it all out with the wind."

I didn't tell him about Leichenbegleiter because it seemed more a problem of psychology than exorcism. Maybe even a problem of psychiatry. After all, the director of our island asylum had said there were two disorders most similar to demonic possession: the syndrome of repressed memories and multiple personalities. Aw, fuck it. I keep on forgetting words and watches, and it's true I'm a Gemini—a schizophrenic sign. The only good thing in all this is that my demon is female, Angina Pectoris, and some day maybe I'll have a roll in the hay with it.

Later on the demons abandoned us, and we talked about normal things. Marijan told me he'd seen Renata and she was well. She was aware of everything but didn't know why she'd dug up her daughter. She had all kinds of excuses, from her little fingernails to her little teeth. But before they found the kid, she'd already been working at the asylum. They'd prescribed her work therapy because at home she thought about nothing but death. She only did physical exams. Perhaps she blurted something out then.

We also talked about the pseudo-Testen. Somebody from the monastery was copying Testen's paintings. He'd begun after

Testen's death and completely dedicated himself to mimicry, like some kind of painting chameleon. That's why now there was a line of gouaches and aquarelles very much like Testen's, and always some wise guy, a researcher or art historian, who claimed he'd discovered a new Testen cycle. As Marijan's recounting all this it seems his mood has improved. I wink at him, but he pretends he doesn't see and goes on to tell me all about the paintings that exist there now. His concern is touching. Just as he's been hiding behind that hurtful name for most of his life, now he's completely huddled behind the colorful mimesis of paint stains. That was probably the origin of the gouaches of the Match Girl, that chronicler of the world using Testen's eyes. So that nothing might be forgotten just because the devil had emerged from oblivion. Surely the name of my next demon will be Alzheimer.

3 TITO'S JAW

The sun's out. It's the third day of my stay at this place over the entrance to which there's an inscription, not "Abandon all hope, ye who enter here" but, as if for camouflage, CARDIOVAS-CULAR DISEASE STATION.

By seven o'clock I was feeling pain above my left temple. This meant the gland above my eyebrow had gotten inflamed, and now when I turned my head it created a dull pain. I'd also lost the view of the back end of that compact nurse whose name, I meanwhile learned, was Marina. Now Marina's a fine name for a woman, but, as far as I'm concerned, it's a much better name for a sebaceous gland. It reminds me of women of the world: Marina Vlady, Marina Tsvetaeva, ladies with charisma, talent, and fatality. Which was why I decided to lend her name to the disobedient bag of puss on my head. I was born with it. It found its place above the thin end of my left eyebrow and at first they didn't call it a sebaceous gland but a cyst. The name had weight: Cystic Marina.

I should probably say my mother fought with that Marina for years, as if it was a wicked daughter-in-law. The showdowns were like this: she sits me on a chair in the kitchen so my left profile is facing the window, for light. Then she ties a white towel around my neck, like for a haircut, and washes her hands thoroughly. I watch her take her rings off so she can wash even the hidden parts of her fingers and palms. She often uses a nail brush. When she's done with her preparations, she bends over me and with her two index fingers squeezes a thick white liquid smelling of mild decomposition from Marina.

So on my head I had this large carbuncle named after a woman, and it kept coming back. Unfortunately, it came back at just this delicate cardiovascular moment, and the compact nurse wanted nothing to do with it. Why should she deal with worldly women when she wasn't paid for it? I could hardly wait for Franka, who arrived some time after all those noons, with fresh fish soup. She was in a hurry, and, as if talking to a small child, announced that we were just going to eat the soup and she'd be going. She had to pack her things. Then I showed her Marina.

She wrapped a napkin around my neck, laid me on the bed gently, still as if dealing with a child, and then in one firm squeeze that revealed the experienced woman in her, forced a large quantity of puss out onto the gauze soaked with alcohol. I felt relief, and she, maybe, passion. Probably the kind of passion that comes to life in puberty when you have to deal with zits. Especially if the zits are large, with little white heads, especially if they squirt onto the mirror. At least there'd been one moment of passion in our long friendship.

She was just bending over me, a cotton pad in her hand, when Mungos showed up. I could only imagine what it all looked like from his perspective. And it made me happy. As soon as he stepped into the room, having seen the action on the bed, he cried out wickedly, "Sorry!" with an unnatural stress on the "o."

Franka was insulted, and I laughed because I knew what he was thinking. She quickly made herself scarce, and Mungos unloaded oranges onto my nightstand. Hospital visitors would die of grief if God hadn't invented oranges and fried chicken. These somehow give them the feeling they've fulfilled their end of the bargain. But Mungos was here on other business.

"Let's go to the doctor's office!" he said. "I brought the tape."

I wasn't sure I was ready for excitement but still went with him. We entered and said hi to Feri, who'd already set up the video and was discretely retreating. Mungos had obviously given him instructions beforehand. Mungos put the tape into the machine, and we got comfortable on the reddish fake-leather armchairs in front of the desk.

First we heard music, but the picture was still just a dark square with a light line in the middle. The sound was poor. Then the picture finally came on. A huge sandy beach without trees. Our Sahara, no doubt. In the distance we saw the contours of Sveti Grgur and Goli Otok. An attractive redhead in a yellow bikini and a saucy thong with too much make-up on her face was playing with a black Schnauzer. She'd throw him a long object and he'd bring it back happily. Every time he dropped the object before her feet, a rubber bone, she patted him on the head and neck. The Schnauzer looked happy.

They played like this for quite a while. A touching friendship between dog and human. Then the girl focused her attention on the Schnauzer's bone. The music changed. It became more dramatic. She spread the beach towel, which until then was hanging around her neck, and lay down on it. She started caressing herself with the long dog bone over her stomach and breasts. The dog stood beside her and drooled, expecting her to throw him the bone. But she liked the bone too. As she removed her top, her large breasts fell out, each to one side. She caressed her nipples with the broader end of the bone, which was supposed to represent a socket. The dog kept on waiting with his tongue hanging out. His eyes, it seemed, showed a certain sadness when the bone ended up on the front side of her bikini.

Then the girl smiled into the camera as if somebody dear to her was behind it, and bent over. She removed the line of her thong, but she didn't take it off. She gave the bone to the dog who licked it, and then she pushed the bone up her anus. She kept on pushing it in and sighed as if masturbating. The dog occasionally joined in with his tongue. I couldn't tell if he did it because of the bone or her ass. They played like this for a while, and then the dog jumped on her.

"Can dogs get gonorrhea?" I asked, wanting to break the tension.

"Ask Vjeko," Mungos said without taking his eyes off the screen. He didn't want to miss anything. This told me it was the first time he'd watched the tape and he hadn't seen it at the police station. He probably had his reasons.

Meanwhile the Schnauzer continued his assaults on her derriere. But something wasn't right. And then I realized the tape didn't show she was a transsexual. She put her legs together and hid her penis so we could only see her voluptuous cheeks and large breasts. In this film they were selling her as a woman. Something she, it seemed, always wanted to be. It was a touching little untruth. Because it was so childish.

When the dog finished, the picture broke up and started shaking, as if the cameraman didn't know how to turn it off. Still on all fours, she was telling him something, but we couldn't understand what. Then the screen went dark for a moment. When the Match Girl appeared on the grayish sand of Sahara again, she was alone. The Schnauzer was gone. She was walking, trying to look sexy, but it all actually reminded me of certain scenes from *The Sound of Music*. As she walked like that, the camera now showed her front and then switched to her back, but none of the scenes revealed her male member. Then she saw something. Something disturbing, you could tell by her face. The something stood in the distance and watched her. When the camera drew nearer, we saw it was a huge snarling lizard, the size of a smaller crocodile. It stood there completely still. Then all of a sudden, from somewhere outside the shot, two men showed up and grabbed the girl. She was unconvincingly trying to break loose while they removed her scarce clothes, paying attention to keep her penis hidden. They forced her to the ground before the lizard, breasts first. The lizard didn't move. She had to lick his snout, which also seemed completely still. Just like crocodiles when you watch them at the zoo. But any second they can attack you with lightning speed. That's what the lizard looked like. It was the biggest monitor lizard I'd ever seen. The next scenes showed a very red animal penis entering her behind. But it was clear the penis belonged to a dog. The scenes had obviously been edited together. In the distance the lizard with its mouth open lay on the girl in the mating position whereas in the close-up the red member penetrated her. Those two men stood on the side and watched as the lizard satisfied itself with the girl. Four strange animals in a mating act.

Mungos stopped the film. "That's Dino. He works at the ferry!" he said, pointing at the taller of the two lizard pimps.

The image of the other one was blurry. He'd turned toward the camera only once, but at that point the sun was right behind him. Shorter, well-built, with a goatee a la d'Artagnan, and straight long hair in back. Probably that friend of mine from Mirna's funeral. But I couldn't tell for sure.

"You know that one?" I asked. Mungos only stared at the screen, rewound the tape several times, but couldn't recognize him.

"All kinds of bastards infesting the island," he said. "Seasonal workers. They wait tables, and then get a little work on the side."

The film stopped abruptly, as if the tape had run out. Or, perhaps, something unexpected had happened before the camera...

Anyhow, we replayed it several times, trying to decide if the lizard was alive or dead. Mungos explained that some time ago in the house that belonged to Captain Baldo Španjol from Supetarska Draga they'd found another large, stuffed monitor lizard like that one. The captain had brought it back from one of his journeys to South America. It was his pet for years, and later the Franciscans from St. Euphemia had stuffed it. But people said he'd brought back two lizards, a couple. Like Noah. So there was a real possibility they had spread over the island and some might have survived even until today.

"That would make the idea she was killed by an animal not so ridiculous," I said.

"The problem is it is ridiculous," Mungos said as he placed a file of papers whose headers I knew well before me. A

Rijeka autopsy report. My fellow pathologist's official opinion excluded animal bites as the cause of death. Death was caused by strangulation, probably with a narrow, elastic object. Her windpipe had been crushed. And the bites were, most likely, postmortem. It was unusual there were no traces of saliva or any other organic material.

A short knock on the door and in walked the nurse. "You have a visitor!" she said. She wanted to see what was on the screen but Mungos stopped the tape.

"Who is it?" I wasn't expecting another visitor today.

"Maskarin and Globus," Mungos said. "I thought you'd be glad."

First of all, and most importantly, Maskarin and Globus had brought a bottle of French cognac.

"Just for medicinal purposes!" Globus explained as he gave me the bottle. "A sip a day, and your veins will be fantastic." He looked much better than two days before, when we'd taken Renata away. Even his hair and beard had grown a little, so he didn't look like an alien anymore. All four of us went to Škver, in front of the lovers' terrace. I threw the striped hospital robe over my back to protect myself from the wind. We took the bottle of medicine along.

"Let's not walk too far, Fero might get hurt," Maskarin said. I was sure he hadn't chipped in to buy the bottle. We sat down on a wall above the beached canoes, which looked like they were dreaming their fall dream out there on the beach and waiting for next season. The evening was clear and very pleasant. I looked at the stars as the bottle circled among us. We all took good gulps, for our health.

At first we avoided any conversation about Renata, but after the bottle had gone round a couple of times, Globus brought it up himself. "I'm really worried, guys," he said, and his voice seemed to have changed somehow. This was supposed to prepare us. "They won't let her out for a long time, you'll see. They say she's well, but what the fuck do they know. It's not their child who died… and they're not the ones who dug it up…"

"Who knows what causes these things?" Maskarin said.

"Fuck, what causes it," Globus replied. "Misery. The worst fuckin' misery you can imagine." He grabbed the bottle for more medicine. "They say she dug her up because… because she wanted to fix something. Guilty conscience…"

Mungos put a hand on his shoulder. "You don't have to torture yourself. We can talk about something else."

"No, I have to. I really do."

And then the Motorola crackled from Mungos' belt. It seemed he never separated from it, not even in moments of tragedy such as this. As if Angina Pectoris and insanity were not enough, we needed something official too. And officialdom came really fast. It took only a couple of words from the other end.

Mungos hung up and stood there in shock for a while. He was so quiet that I thought there had been another tragedy.

"Well? What's up?" Maskarin said, the least patient of us.

Globus only lifted his head in resignation. "They've arrested Muki!" Mungos finally managed to utter. This was enough for another long silence.

Globus put his face in his hands, and we could see his shoulders were shaking.

"They found something of his at the crime scene. Hair, epithelia, something like that. I was convinced it was that bastard from the Imperial," Mungos said. "He was into saws. And what's poor Muki's fault? It burned him when he peed is all."

Globus cried harder and harder. The captain of the island police offered him the bottle, and he took it. His face was producing a lot of moisture, which made the neck of the bottle wet. And then he said, after a long silence, "I did her… that bitch! Muki's innocent."

We all sat there in shock. It occurred to me all this had happened because of too much of that medicine—we'd drunk half the bottle in no time. But Mungos was interested in something else.

"Did you fuck her too?" he said in a raspy voice in which there was still hope and hugged him, here on Škver, next to the canoes where the lovers usually come. "Everybody around here's a great Catholic and a stallion. The whole island's full of them. But scratch the surface just a little and you can't get away from faggots."

After his question, there was expectant silence. In the end, despite his crime, Globus was still on our side. "I didn't fuck her!" he said. "I didn't fuck her!"

We were all somehow relieved. We thought he was still clean, just like he'd been at school, clean and honest, whatever that meant in these circumstances. And then, through that slobber of his, he added, "But she gave me a blowjob!"

Mungos' world suddenly collapsed. He tried to control his sadness. And maybe his anger too. Because it would've been easier for us all if our childhood friend had stayed on this side of the fortress, among us, the heteros and proud of it, I don't know why.

"Okay," Mungos said, "tell me because I want to know, and later we'll see."

I didn't miss the fact that he glanced around to see if any bystanders were listening. True the lawyer was present, but maybe the cognac had distorted his legal sense.

"I don't give a fuck," Globus said. "I strangled her with my lucky fishing rod!"

"Your fishing rod?"

"You remember my big fishing rod with the Camel sticker on it. I made a braid. That's how you strengthen the line. You take three threads and braid them together just like little girls do with their hair."

Here he was overtaken by tears again. Probably because he remembered the hair, which was now after a short and false resurrection below ground again. He spat, got up, and washed the salty tears in the sea. Water in water, salt in salt.

"What were you thinking about when you strangled her?" Mungos asked, wanting to help him somehow.

"About the alphabet!"

Mungos was quiet. You could tell it wasn't easy for him. Globus either.

"She had just learned the Croatian alphabet. Written and printed both. So I was repeating to myself: 'ABC... ČĆD... I remember I didn't know which one came first, Č or Ć. Mirna knew."

I suddenly felt Globus' grief was somehow greater because of these letters, as if the death of a child who knew the alphabet was harder to get over.

"I had to let her lick me, so I could slip a noose around her neck..."

"And when did you shave," Mungos pounced, trying to help him. "Before or after?"

Globus laughed in the middle of all this mess. It was very cynical laughter.

"Before! I was a fool... I didn't want to leave my hair at the scene of..."

"The strangulation," Mungos put in compassionately.

Then he laughed again and kept on repeating how he didn't care anymore. It crossed my mind that perhaps this was what

Renata had wanted to fix. To dig up?

"I was crying. Muki was driving me in his boat and I must have told him everything. I don't remember anymore. He took the jaw of that shark we'd caught in the canal at Dolin, the day before Tito's visit. That's why we called it Tito. Only its jaw survived. And then he fixed her a little."

He paused. Probably to remove all that water that kept pouring out all the orifices in his face.

"Yeah, and as she was blowing me, I thought about how I'd never jerked off either in elementary school or in high school. I was saving myself for true love, fuck! I was a priest to myself." Then he blew a gob of spit toward the sea, but a portion of it remained on his chin for irony's sake. "Is this what you get in return for purity? God!"

He asked this theological question just before he started to vomit, releasing semi-digested food onto his sandals, and, if I'm not mistaken, wiggling his toes.

4 ST. CLARE'S RAIN

I remained sitting above the canoes, wearing my pajamas and slippers, like a sleepwalking philosopher. Maskarin and Mungos had taken Globus to sleep. Probably so he wouldn't confess anything else. Anyhow, even this was more than enough. Except for one little thing: why had he strangled the Match Girl? That he hadn't explained. Stipe Striptiz at least had good reasons for what he did. Anyone who rents out their purebred best friend for porn can expect something unpredictable. And this canine-transsexual story took a rather unpleasant turn. As soon as he found out about the nature of Marillena's injuries, he decided to get rid of the dog. Maybe the fool thought the Schnauzer had ripped her throat in a moment of passion. This would mean he didn't take part in the filming. He killed the animal, buried it, and when he heard the tape was making the rounds, decided to dig up the dog and hide him somewhere safe. Probably in some freezer with tooth fish and sea bass. So it could wait for the next season, and so the police dogs wouldn't find it. The resurrected island Schnauzer, which the children had spent days looking for in order to give it a decent burial, had probably ended up on ice. Like Walt Disney.

Then I felt somebody leaning on my shoulder. It was Franka. "I was looking for you in your room. Aren't you cold here?"

I wanted to tell her I was only cold around my heart, on the inside, while on the outside this hospital robe with number 11 on it—like on a soccer player's back—kept me warm just fine.

I was about to ask what she was doing here, but she was faster. "I've packed my bags! I came to say goodbye!"

At that moment in the sky over the town a shooting-star suddenly appeared.

"Make a wish!" she chirped as if she was suddenly a little girl again. And as if my Angina and her clawed animal had retreated to one of their previous stages. But I was appaled. How could this be happening again?

"You have to make a wish, but you mustn't tell. You know how it goes!" she said. "Let's walk a little. I'm cold."

We got up and walked down Škver toward Vela Stina. Franka was talking about her plans for the future. She was toying with the idea of opening her own video store where she'd keep classics. Fellini, Bergman, de Sica. She said she'd had enough of those council books and Maskarin's family connections.

184

"Give me a little of that robe of yours," she said suddenly. "I'm freezing!"

I took off my robe and put it around both of us. I felt her whole body shaking. And then, to my alarm, another shooting-star appeared in the sky.

"This one's mine," she said. "Now I'll make a wish!"

It looked like somebody big up above us was striking matches and with every one, at least for a moment, prolonging our lives on this cold night.

After another bright star burned out above the central part of the bay, we saw a blind man. He was walking toward us carefully, led by a black Labrador with a white harness around his chest. I was just wondering why blind men's gear was always white, and their guide dogs black, when Franka said, "That's our old guest, from Belgium. He comes here every fall and often goes for walks here in the park. Aren't they sweet?"

She was obviously still under the influence of the stars. And it crossed my mind that the dog might have taken him to the cemetery while the concrete was still soft. The poor Belgian had had no idea he'd found himself at the place of ultimate repose, which was inappropriate for dogs. That's probably how that print had ended up there. Maybe some woman might have seen him there while she was visiting her late husband's grave, but she wouldn't have had the heart to tell him he was being inconsiderate. He was blind, he didn't know what he was doing. She, poor thing, was full of Christian compassion, but deep down in her soul she just couldn't forgive him. To make things worse, the dog had peed on her husband's grave, and she was still a pretty widow in her prime, with tits, thighs, and everything else in place amid her tight mourning dress. Maybe she resented the fact he was blind and couldn't see how pretty she was, not that his dog had peed on her husband's grave.

"What are you thinking about?" Franka chirped. "There's another one. God, as if it's August. These meteor showers usually happen in August, I read somewhere. This year they're calling it St. Clare's Rain."

I wanted to tell her to say all this to the Poor Clares, maybe they'd start speaking. But I didn't. Instead I asked, "What's the story with you and... Baldie?"

She held me closer. Probably because she was cold.

"I've lived with him for years," she said. "You know, on and off."

"And nobody on the island knows?"

"When his wife was alive, I went there to have coffee. After she died, I helped him with the countess."

Another star cut through the sky, this one so exceptionally bright that it seemed it was falling from the town walls. That was what I was afraid of.

"I didn't tell you about it because I thought you, well... thought something like this too. You were always so shy before, you never said anything."

And even if I had, I thought, you wouldn't have understood because we'd probably be standing in the middle of some loud noise. Better I didn't say anything. Let the most passionate thing between us be that squeezing of the sebaceous gland. Now I needed to tell her something else. Something important.

"Fuck it, all this time I was afraid you were a virgin. That's what people said. And I was always afraid of one image. That you'd die and end up on the autopsy table like that, and the pathologist, some bastard, would pierce that little skin with his finger. And say something to make his students laugh."

Usually it's weights that fall from people's minds, but that evening it wasone incredibly heavy hymen that fell from mine.

Together with the stars of St. Clare, which grew brighter and brighter.

"You don't have to be afraid of that anymore," she said and kissed me next to my ear. Almost like a friend.

There was something erotic in it. Like a man getting a hard on for his own mother.

"Tomorrow I'm going to the hospital," she said suddenly. "To have my chemotherapy. I want to kill everything crawling inside me."

Then she saw more bright shiny stars. We'd just reached the stairs that lead from Škver to Piazzetta.

"This is coming from town," she said. "It looks like fireworks."

"Please," I said. "You don't want to see that."

But she'd already flown up Gornja Street toward the little square next to St. Mary's Church, which was where it was coming from.

The scene I'd witnessed with Renata fifteen years before was replayed. A couple of boys from the town were sitting on the wall near the Poor Clares Monastery. They had a cage with sparrows. One of them would take a bird out, dip its head and wings in gasoline, set it on fire, and let it fly. The bird would then flutter its wings, cheeping horribly, as if wanting to put out that blaze, and then splash into the sea below town. From down there they looked just like shooting stars.

Midnight Tolls and Tolls

It's pitch dark outside. Not even the stars are falling anymore, and some evil-minded soldier on leave has used his gun to switch off the street lamp on the boardwalk before the police station. Mungos and I now rely on the twinkling light of a naked bulb that hangs from the ceiling on a wire in one of the offices on the first floor of the station. He's sitting behind a green, prehistoric Olympia typewriter, while I occupy the chair reserved for suspects on the other side of the desk. I look at the map of the world on the wall behind the chief. There's a crucifix above it. Just so we know who created it.

The two of us are writing an official report. The crime team from Rijeka has disappeared into the unknown. Probably in search of fresh corpses. At least those are abundant these days. Yesterday they received a mysterious call informing them of some big crime, so they loaded their stuff into the vans in a panic and headed straight for Lika. Meanwhile, Mungos promoted me as if he were making me a knight. But instead of a sword he placed his right hand on my shoulder and informed me in a friendly voice that now I was the official pathologist in the Little Match Girl case and we had to write a report. And we two knights took a seat at the desk in the empty office and got down to business. It was like we were composing one of those endings Maskarin had ripped out from the island library's books.

"Fuck, I don't know where to begin," Mungos complained, his two fingers doing a ten hut above the keyboard. "I didn't know how to do it even when we were at school. Intro, body, conclusion. Fuck that. I'd always write it ten minutes before the deadline."

"Why don't you just say it, we'll write it later. Don't worry about it," I say. But I'm burning with curiosity because, well, I got sick at the worst time. Globus' confession came unexpectedly. And I was a little suspicious. It seemed he was protecting somebody. But then again, you don't confess a murder just like that, from pure altruism. You have to have strong reasons.

Meanwhile, Mungos poured me a shot of Pelinkovac. Probably so I could brace myself for the unexpectedly tragic circumstances. Or whatever they were.

"We won't write this down yet," he said. "I want you to have the whole picture. First of all, this lab report from Rijeka isn't worth shit."

"How come?" The autopsy report was signed by a colleague from the Zagreb forensic lab. He sometimes stopped in at Rijeka too. Part-time. Especially when there was work. I didn't know what was wrong with that.

"It doesn't say anything specific. First, the injuries on the little buttfuck are without a doubt caused by an animal. But then, since they found no traces of saliva or anything else indicating an animal, they can't conclude the death was caused by an animal. Besides, her windpipe was crushed, like she was strangled. Still, maybe it's possible she was strangled by this animal. Some unknown animal... A little tape would do a lot of good here."

"I don't get it," I said. We knew very well the injuries came from the shark's jaw. Even more, from the Blue Shark that was caught for the Marshall at Dolin a day before the presidential yacht sailed into the harbor.

"What?" Mungos said, somewhat agitated. "Or are you just playing dumb with me?"

"I don't get it," I repeated. But maybe I did and just wanted him to say it.

"Put it this way. It would be extremely practical for all of us if it turned out to be an animal. You're a supervisor here now. Why don't you just write, 'Animal!' See, you can add it right here."

He pushed the pathology report under my nose.

"You want me to falsify an official document?"

"I want you to write your opinion. Who's going look at it now. In the middle of this fucking war! One animal more or less…"

"So that's why you've been dragging me around all this time!" I said, but without anger. Just so he understood.

Mungos made the kind of face you make when you're talking to a small child, coaxing him into something simple and obvious. Then he poured himself a shot. Probably to fortify his long lost rhetorical skills.

I said, "First give me a reason. If it's Globus, I want to know why! Why would the most moral person I know strangle a Romanian hooker?"

"What do you mean 'if'? You were there when he said he did it. What else do you need?"

"I don't know. I just think it's strange."

Mungos appeared not to have heard my last remark. He was lost in thought in front of that map as if the whole world was pressing down on his shoulders or he was creating it all over again. But actually he was thinking about something else.

"Ok, I'll give you the whole story," he said, giving in. "And you decide for yourself!"

You decide meant, do you want to put your childhood

friend in danger? Stick blindly to the facts or correct them a bit? Just enough to preserve the contours of your alternate homeland? And keep our soccer team together?

Then he went on, "Do you remember that box with SECURITATE written on it? We found it in the kid's room."

"I remember," I said, thinking, where's he going with this?

"Do you know why it was so heavy?" he says, looking into my face as if trying to read something there. And then, "Because the sides were full of led. What do you carry in led boxes?"

I shake my head.

"Radioactive things. Uranium, plutonium. That kind of shit."

"On the red muslin?"

"Well, that's what's most interesting. It's all that Jungwirth's fault. You know the one who treated Mirna. He's Tomo's cousin."

"I didn't know he was Tomo's cousin," I say, surprised.

"He is," Mungos says as if for a moment I've caught him on the wrong foot, "some distant cousin. They weren't very close. Until that kid of his was born."

"The moron?"

"Retarded," he corrects me, like he's suddenly been injected with a shot of kindness. "He was telling Tomo they should put her in a home. To make their lives easier, have more children. But they didn't want to hear about it. Actually Tomo was against it. And right about that time he became friends with the Match Girl. Do you know what kind of a friendship it was?"

"He was her lover," I say. "She wanted to have an operation because of him. I told you that!"

"Eh, no!" Mungos says cheerfully, as if he's happy I'm mistaken all the time. "Their friendship involved… business. But not what you think, sucking and all that… a hand here, a tongue there, anyway… Jungwirth doesn't have gonorrhea. He needed her for other things. He knew what was up in Romania when Ceausescu was on his way down. The man read the papers, watched TV. Later he even studied some books. I know, I was at his place. I found them there."

"What?"

"The books. On Romania. He knew what the Securitate did. I asked him, 'Are you studying communist regimes?' 'No, no,' he says, 'Just reading. I'm interested in their kind of writing.' I tell myself, 'Fuck me if you're interested in regimes and literature. Like you really want to know something about Romania. Transylvania, Dracula, and all that, my ass! A modern day Dracula, that's who you are!'"

"Come on, tell me already!" I say, curious because everything he's said is making sense. He's only a little mistaken about the cousin, though maybe that's true too.

"The thing is Ceausescu was just like Stalin. He had this need, from time to time, to get rid of his associates. Close comrades from the government or the Central Committee. And you can't do this without creating a scandal, I mean, fuck it, they're all well-known comrades. Especially in the last fifteen years. So he gave them watches as presents. In those boxes, on red muslin. And he even had an inscription put in the gilding: 'To comrade so and so, in token of our friendship and gratitude…' And inside the watches, of course, there's radioactive plutonium. And the victim, suspecting nothing, wears the presidential watch like the highest decoration. Then his health starts deteriorating. First, just a little: fatigue, perspiration, blood tests come out fine. Not enough iron. The doctors say, 'Eat beats. Have a glass of red wine after dinner.' Six months later the devoted comrade is gone. Leukemia. The president cries before his coffin. They've been comrades ever since their youth. I mean, they fought in the fucking revolution together. And now one's lying in a coffin."

"So what are you saying? That Jungwirth…"

"Got this watch from Marillena. Stipe told us she went to Romania. When she came back she was loaded. Jungwirth bought it from her. God knows who she fucked for that box. Besides, after the revolution they sell this stuff like cheese, on the street almost. Just like our Gypsies yell 'Watches! Watches!' all the time, they say 'Watches!' too, but these are radioactive. For your friends and family. Well, he showed the watch to Tomo. Together with the box. She already had the earring. She could have the watch too. He explained everything to him. Clean and discrete… in six months. No one on the island would suspect anything. Death wouldn't even be painful, you just shut down."

"And Tomo said yes!?"

"Why on earth would he do that? Kill his own child? People here are not like that. He told him, 'Fuck you and your watch!' So Jungwirth returned it to Marillena."

"Did she give him back the money?"

"I don't know if he asked for it. But it's possible he told Bobo. The writer."

"He was on the waiting list too?"

Mungos paused to think for a moment, as if he'd lost the thread. The waiting list must have confused him. Then he said, "You mean for the watch? Maybe. But the tape showed up with Bobo, the watch didn't. He claims he didn't watch it. I believe him. Something's screwed up here. I haven't solved that part yet. He probably likes these things out of pure writerly curiosity."

"How come… you haven't solved it?" I said.

"Well, I haven't figured out," he said, "how it all happened."

"Where's the watch?" This was the key question. There were all kinds of boxes, but the only real piece of evidence was the watch.

Mungos too sensed this was the key question because he suddenly grew listless and somewhat uncertain, and said, "Well, we haven't found the watch yet. But it's just a question of time…"

Of course it's a question of time, I thought. And the watch is nowhere in sight. Who knows whose time it's ticking now? Tomo might have something to say about that. Or Jungwirth. But they wouldn't say anything because this whole thing was an attempted murder and you go to prison for that. But there were holes.

"And what about the murder? How does the strangled Match Girl fit into all this?"

"Well, see, it was a misunderstanding. Marillena lived two houses away from Globus and Renata. Their kid sometimes played at her place. Of course, her parents didn't know about it. She even taught her some Romanian. You've heard what Marijan said. I trust him."

This I could picture. Two girls becoming close. Mirna trying on her large high heels. The stories of Transylvania.

"And Mirna probably liked taking other people's things," Mungos went on carefully. You mustn't speak ill of the dead. But if you must say anything ill, something a little less ill will do. It sounds better.

"A kleptomaniac?"

"She found the box. She was a kid. She liked it. Gold with red muslin. A watch inside."

"And Globus thought Marillena gave it to her. She killed his child. A father can't accept the fact that his six-year old daughter, his angel, might be a kleptomaniac, stealing from other people's houses. He scraped off his hair so he wouldn't leave any trace behind. He knew one hair would be enough. Then he braided up his lucky fishing line."

Things fit, all the details. The scorched cricket belonged to Mirna. There were other toys there that hadn't ended up in her little white coffin. Then the gilded box. Only the killer watch was missing. Perhaps in the report we could write the suspected Seiko had skipped town. Globus must have found out about the watch and realized what had happened. But it was too late. The kid was already in Jungwirth's jurisdiction. How did the Leichenbegleiter wannabe feel treating the little girl who'd practically died by his hand? Even if he wasn't the one who'd killed her, it was he who had summoned the devil. Like the mother from that poem who brought the plague to the village. Her sadness was most tragic of all.

But the complications didn't sit well. We still hadn't found Marillena's lover. Police reports are usually much simpler. Who was he? Not Jungwirth. Globus? In this case Mirna wasn't the motive. Besides, who was Globus protecting with his confession? Muki? Because he hoped we were still friends? That I'd give him and my home another chance? After all, Mirna worked best as a motive because she helped people understand the murderer. And identify with him. Mungos had guessed well. But these same facts could, perhaps, add up to a different story.

"Now you've heard it all! You know everything. Have you made up your mind?" he said, pushing those coroner's papers under my nose. But he was clearly thinking, "What's one animal more or less among all the animals in this zoo?" The pen was just there. Maybe it was one of those lost pens now, only for a moment, returned from pen heaven. Or hell, maybe. That would be more appropriate since I needed to sign with it. And the thing is that a couple of hours before, while I'd been think-ing about things mystical, I somehow had the feeling that in the end I'd have to sign something. I just didn't know what form it would take.

Meanwhile, Mungos is trying to make it easier on me. Just as he did for Globus when Globus confessed his sins in that drunken stupor with the even drunker lawyer nearby.

"Besides, he just got his draft papers," he says, looking at me to see what kind of impact he's created. He's working on me psychologically, psychiatrically. I can almost hear him say-ing, 'Our justice is nearsighted. Let destiny deal with it.' But he doesn't say that. He doesn't want to go that far. And I begin to weigh things, like the blind goddess of justice. I weigh and calculate, and this is the first step toward that dark place.

If I leave my home intact and put my signature under ani-mal death and everything stays as it is, I'll be able to come back here. If not, I'll never set foot on these shores again. And if my old friend happens to become a war hero, I'll be a traitor to boot. Then the only thing I'll be fit for is selling my house and never showing up here again. I'll sell it and all the paintings and books with it. The books are dangerous anyhow. Maybe I could take the doormat. Cleanse myself on it through and through. Maybe even put it before my own grave.

I look at the pen, calculating. The bells begin to strike mid-night. I have the feeling they'll keep ringing. Because a town with four noons must have even more midnights. And in the end they'll swallow each and every one of us.